Tarnished

By

Alexander Acevedo

ISBN

Hardcover: 978-1-965560-55-6

Paperback: 978-1-965560-56-3

DEDICATION

I would like to dedicate this book to my friends and my family.

ABOUT THE AUTHOR

My name is Alexander Acevedo, and I wrote this story during my deployment in Iraq. While I don't intend to turn it into a series, I envision it as part of a larger universe where other stories will intersect with Tarnished. My goal with this story was to create something that both busy adults and teens could dive into and get lost in, even during their hectic lives. I sincerely hope you enjoy the world I've crafted, and I'd love your support in sharing it with others so they can enjoy it, too.

Contents

CHAPTER 1

The moment my eyes flickered open, my head ached like I was hit by a bat. It was dead silent in the room I was in, and it smelled like perfume and weed. Not a bad combination. I thought. I lifted myself up with my left arm; my right hand was pressed against my throbbing head. Looking around, I realized I had no clue where I was. The room was small and dirty, with dingy white walls splattered with graffiti, like some sort of urban art gone wrong. The floor was completely covered with clothes to the point where I couldn't see the floor.

I was covered by a thick, red and black blanket. The fabric of the blanket was slightly scratchy against my back. Pushing the covers off, I noticed that I was absolutely naked. Groaning, I swung my legs over the sidhe of the bed, my bare feet hitting the cold floor. I see my clothes lying in a small pile near the wall. I pick them up and throw my shirt on the bed while I slip on my favorite slim-fitting black jeans with one of the knees blown out. I zipped up my pants, and as the silver button slid through the hole in my jeans, the door swung open, and I walked a total knockout.

She was a stone-cold fox with a playful smile that lit up the dim room.

"Hey, you're up," she said, her voice was smooth like honey.

"Ha yeah, my head is killing me," I winced from the pain.

"I bet you had a big night," she giggled as she walked over to a nightstand near the bed.

"Where am I?" I groaned while I pulled my baby blue v-neck over my head.

"You're at my place in the Grove," she replied casually, her eyes sparkling with mischief. She tossed me a white bottle with no label.

"Take two of those. You'll feel better in no time."

I fumbled with the childproof lid at first, and when I finally got it open, I dumped two bright blue pills onto my hand.

"Are these oxy's? Fuck it," I muttered, slamming them into my mouth and washing them down with a gulp of saliva. I stopped and looked at this total babe in front of me. She was damn near perfect. She had orange back-length hair with black highlights, black and white gauges in her ears, and tattoos that covered both of her arms and both of her legs. My pants grew tight when I peeked at what she got on. This goddess was wearing a sleeveless band tee from my personal favorite band, *Catfish and the Bottlemen*, paired with short black cut-off jeans that hugged her curves just right.

"So, what happened last night?" I said as I put on my black slip-on shoes.

"Well, I met you at the Lucky Suns concert, and you were pretty gone already." She explained. Her smile was wide and welcoming.

"I'm sorry about that," I said, feeling of wave embarrassment within me. She laughs and lays down on the bed.

"Don't be. You don't have to apologize for having a good time." Her laughter echoed in the room.

Just then, I felt the pills kick in, and it made me feel light and untouchable. I sat on the corner of the bed and turned my head towards her.

"You're gonna think I'm a dick, but I can't remember your name," I admitted, my cheeks flushing slightly.

She came from behind, kissed me on the cheek, slid around, and sat on my lap facing me.

"My name is Tesa Youth, but you call me Tes," she smiled.

As I stared into her deep chocolate eyes, I found myself completely lost in the moment. I leaned in for a kiss, feeling a rush of warmth.

"I'm Michael," I said with a grin on my face.

She kissed me and said, "I know, silly."

Her arms wrapped around my neck. I grabbed her thighs and effortlessly stood as I stood.

"You wanna get breakfast?" I grinned again.

"I'm game," she said as she hopped down.

She threw on a pair of black and white vans, and we headed out into the living room. There was a couple on the couch, and a guy passed out underneath a glass coffee table that had a bunch of records on it.

One of the records had a small pile of white gold on it and a few lines already cut up.

"Don't worry about them," she laughed, grabbing my hand and leading me out of the house.

CHAPTER 2

Stepping outside felt amazing; the sun was out, but it wasn't too hot, and a refreshing breeze felt so good against my dry skin. Tes locked the door and turned towards me, smiling.

"Where do you want to eat?" She asked, her eyes were sparkling.

"We're in the grove, right? Let's go to Auntie's Diner," I suggested, feeling my stomach growl at the thought of good food.

"Damn, good choice," she smiled. Her warmth was contagious.

The Grove was like any small subsection of a city, except it was full of amazing art in every building.

Most of it was done by some unknown artist who went by the name of "ZERO-G." I liked to think that ZERO-G was just some ordinary dude who worked in an office and let out his artistic side in his free time. Besides the stunning art, The Grove is also known for Auntie's Diner. Auntie's Diner looked like it was right out of the 50's. It had the classic metallic siding that gleamed in the sun. The neon lights glowed brightly at night, making it a drunken haven for anyone looking for a late-night bite. The food was always on point, and the jukebox had some killer tunes that always made you want to dance.

As we walked, we shot the shit; the world was buzzing around us.

"So, the graffiti on the walls in your room, did you do that?" I asked as we passed a colorful art.

"Ha, yeah. It's stupid, I know," she said modestly.

"It's not stupid, it's rad as fuck. The combinations of colors, and just the way it comes together, is mind-blowing," I said as we passed a brick building with the words *"**Black Kettle**"* spray painted across it.

She kissed me on the cheek and said, "You're so sweet, honestly; even last night when you were all messed up, you said and did the sweetest things."

I gave her a half smile.

"When we get to Aunties can you fill me in on what happened last night, beautiful?" I laughed.

She winked at me, "I sure can, handsome."

She hooked her arm around mine and moved closer to me as we walked down the sidewalk. Our steps were in sync.

The sky was as blue as the Pacific Ocean, not a cloud in sight, making a day feel perfect.

As we rounded the corner I asked, "Who were those people that were passed out in your living room?"

"Oh, those were my roommates. The two on the couch were Macy and Teddy. Don't call him Teddy, though; he hates it. He goes by Ted, and the dude under the table is Tiger. We actually don't know his real name, but we don't care. I have one more roommate, Heather, but she's at work." She explained, her voice was full of amusement.

"Were they at the concert too?" I inquired, curious about the night's wild adventures.

"Yeah, they were wild as hell. I'll tell you about it when we get inside." Her eyes were glittering with mischief.

We finally reached the parking lot of Auntie's and we walked up to the door and went inside.

CHAPTER 3

Inside of Auntie's we stop at the front and wait to be seated. It's a little bit chilly inside, and I wish I had my hoodie with me. I can see that Tes is cold, too. The bar wraps around the inside, and there are booths along the walls.

At the bar, there are silver stools with red cushions. The place is pretty empty except for a couple sitting in one of the booths and a man with a red trucker hat at the bar. The air was filled with the smell of pancakes, and it made me happy. A blonde woman in her late thirties, wearing a fluorescent pink uniform and white kicks, walked up to us and smiled at both of us.

"Good afternoon, Tes," she said.

"Hey, Pattie," Tes replied, hugging her. Pattie glanced at me quickly.

"How do you know Michael?" She asked Tes.

"I met him last night at the concert I told you about. How do you know Michael?" she laughed.

I hugged Pattie. "Pattie, here is my mother," I said, laughing. "She's the one who surprised me with a ticket for the show last night."

We both looked at my mother, and she said, "What? It was a coincidence."

She laughed, grabbed both of our hands and walked us to a booth in her section. Tes still had a surprised look on her face as we took our seats. My mother handed us our big-for-no-reason menus.

"Don't worry about the bill, you two; it's on me."

"No, ma. I can't let you do that; I'll pay for us."

Tes cuts in. "Uhm, I'll pay for myself," she laughed.

I winked at her and asked for coffee.

"I'll have coffee too, please," said Tes while handing the menu back to her; I handed back my menu too.

"Coming right up."

She turned and disappeared behind a door that was near the bar.

"I can't believe Pattie's your mom. I mean, I've been coming to Auntie's since I was a little girl."

"Crazy how life works sometimes," I winked at Tes and smiled.

"So, I'm pretty sure my mom wanted us to meet," I laughed.

"You think so?" She giggled softly.

"When I was little, my father would take me here every Friday, and I'd get the same thing every time: pancakes, eggs, and orange juice," she told me, her voice softening.

"Sounds like a nice tradition."

"It was," she said, just as my mom reappeared with two steaming mugs of coffee.

"Thank you, Pattie," Tes said as she pulled the coffee closer to her.

"No problem, Dear. Oh, Michael, your father wants you to come visit; he misses you."

I rolled my eyes, "Yeah, right, but tell him I'll stop by on Tuesday."

"Okay, Pumpkin, I will."

My mom nodded, then looked between us with a smile, "Are you two ready to order?"

"I'm ready. Are you, Tes?" I asked, turning to Tes.

"Yeah, I'll have pancakes and eggs."

"Me too," I added.

As my mom jotted down our order, her eyes lit up.

"Wait Pumpkin… Pumpkin... Why does that ring a bell?" She mused.

"Well, you used to hang out here on Fridays when you came in with your dad. You two were so cute." She explained with a chuckle.

"No way," I laughed, shaking my head in disbelief.

"I guess our meeting again was meant to be," Tes smiled at me and touched my hand.

Mom smiled and disappeared again.

"Wow, I can't believe that," I say dumbfounded.

"Oh, last night..." she blurted out, kind of startling me a little bit.

"Yes, tell me about last night." I perked up, intrigued.

"So I don't know what you did before we ran into each other, but I remember everything after," she said, her face lighting up.

"Haha, okay."

"Okay, so the opening band, Fryerman, just finished their set; they killed it, and I was already a little bit tipsy. I wanted another drink, so I and my friends were heading to the bar when this douchebag, with a red snapback and 'Cool Story Babe' t-shirt, tried to hit on me, calling me 'babe' and 'sweetie.' I told him to 'beat it,' but he started to get all handsy, grabbing my wrist. I shouted for him to stop, and then my friends shouted louder. Then, out of nowhere, you came flying out of the crowd, like a sexy knight, and punched him in the face and threw him away from me and told him to 'fuck off."

I grinned, shaking my head. "That guy had it coming."

"He ran away cursing. I could tell that you'd been drinking and maybe messed up on some other things. You looked so damn hot with those tattoos and short black hair pushed up in the front. I thanked you and asked if you wanted to get a drink with me. I think you thought I was asking you to buy me a drink because when we got to the bar, you threw down a 50 and said, 'Double rum and coke, and whatever the beautiful girl wants."

I couldn't help but laugh. "Did I really say that?"

"It made me blush. I took your hand and asked if you wanted to hang out after the show, and you said absolutely and then we split ways for the rest of the Lucky Sons set.

I was hoping you wouldn't forget about me. On the way out, I saw you smoking a cig by the door. I playfully bump into you, and you smile and take my hands as you ask me if I'm ready to go.

"I remember that part," I added.

You put the biggest smile on my face. And I said, "Yes."

"You took an Uber with me and my friends. Five minutes into the ride, you guys were trying to start a band. When we got to my house, we went straight into my room. We started kissing, but when I said I wanted to have sex with you, you said you didn't want to have sex because I had been drinking."

I blinked, trying to take it all in. "I said that?"

"No guy has ever done that, and then you passed out. You got naked in your sleep, but I didn't mind," she winked at me while I picked my jaw up from the ground.

"Hell of a night," I said.

"You can say that again," she giggled.

Looking over, I saw my mother coming with our food. As she arrived, she set down our food in front of us.

"Careful, it's hot," she grinned and kissed me on the cheek.

"Mom." I groaned though I couldn't help but smile.

"You're still my son, no matter how much you get embarrassed," she teased before disappearing again.

Tes giggled and took a bite of her eggs. Mom disappeared again. I wasn't really hungry anymore because of the pills. I felt like I was on top of the world. I stared at Tes and began to daydream.

I snapped out of it when Tes looked at her phone and said, "Fuck, I totally forgot..."

"What's up?" I asked, sitting up straighter.

"I completely spaced, man; I'm supposed to cover for this girl, Taylor, at work."

Without thinking, I said, "I can give you a ride if you want."

"Really?" She asked, her smile growing.

"Yeah. My car must be at my place, but I can borrow my mom's car for an hour. Where do you work?"

"Thanks, and I work at Monics," she replied, looking relieved.

As my mom walked by, I caught her hand.

"Hey, ma, can I borrow the car to take Tes to work?"

"Of course," she said without hesitation, "Just bring it back by nine."

"Okay, ma," I said, feeling grateful.

I threw a 50 down and asked Tes if she was ready to go.

She took one last bite, standing up with a smile, "Yeah, let's hit it."

Mom tossed me the keys on the way out, and we headed to the car.

CHAPTER 4

My mom's car was kinda like that, the car that gets used to drive friends around. It was an old 1995 white mercury sable. I called her "Old reliable." The inside has a grey interior, and it smells like French fries and stale cigs. Hanging from the rearview mirror was a worn Stitch doll I'd won for my mom at the Clover Fair when I was twelve. He had seen better days; his left ear was missing, and his fur was a little frayed. There was no radio, so I rigged it to play tapes from an old Walkman I found in the attic. The front seat had beads that were supposed to help your back, but it was super uncomfortable, in my opinion.

I unlocked my side with the key and reached over to unlock her side. As she opened the door and slid in, I turned the key in the ignition, but the car hesitated and sputtered, refusing to start.

Tes looked over as she shut the door, "Everything okay?"

"Yeah, you just need to give her a little veness from time to time."

I tried again, and this time, the engine roared to life. Music started blaring through the speakers, and I didn't want to waste my time... It startled me, and I turned it down as quickly as I could.

Tes laughed and turned it back up. It made me smile. I backed up and started to drive to Monics.

Tes was singing along. That moment was so perfect. We stopped at a traffic light and saw my friend, Luke, walking with that girl that I would call "a scab." I honked at him, and he jumped and flipped me off. When he noticed it was me, he laughed.

As I pulled away from the light, Tes slid her hand over to grab mine.

"Whatcha doin' gorgeous?" I asked, glancing over at her briefly.

She grinned and pulled a pen from her purse.

"Drawing," she laughed.

I kept my eyes on the road and felt the pen against my skin. I felt her soft hands rubbing on mine. It made me hard as a rock. I adjusted myself by moving my legs. As we arrived at the plaza where Monics was, she finished drawing on me. I stopped the car in front of the store.

She kissed my cheek. "Thanks for the ride, handsome."

"My pleasure, beautiful," I replied, trying to play it cool.

As she opened the door to leave, she looked back, "Call me tonight around 10; I'll be done by then."

"But don't have your number, though." I blinked, realizing I didn't have her number.

She flashed me a mischievous smile, "Check your hand," she said as she ran into the store.

I looked down, and there was her number and her name drawn in tough graffiti style.

CHAPTER 5

Since I had the car for a couple of hours, I decided to go to my pad in the Hollow to shit, shower, and shave. The Hollow was about five minutes south of the Grove, but it felt like another world. The Hollow was like the rich part of the city; the grass was greener, the trees that still stand were tall, and the houses looked like they'd come straight out of some architect's daydream. As I pulled up to the house, I noticed my car wasn't in the driveway.

Fuccckkkkkk, that means it was at Jimmy's house. Fuck it, I'd deal with it later. I pulled into the drive and got out of the car. As I was walking up to my door, my sexy-ass neighbor waved to me. Her name was Natasha; she had long blonde hair, a thick body frame, and a nice pair of tits. She was one of those rich girls that fit the stereotype. She always wore pink, and she was always on her phone. Damn, did she get me hard, though, every time I saw her?

I waved back as I unlocked the door and walked inside. The house was left to me by my real father, Martin Wilder, when he OD'ed. He was a rock star who knocked up a waitress and never met his kid because he was on the road all the time. He was in a band called Master Exploder.

They played hair metal and were huge. Up until I found out, I thought that Frank was my real dad; it kinda explains why he was such a dick to me. When my real dad OD'ed, his lawyer contacted my mother, and she was forced to tell me. It turned out Martin left me everything in his will. In the will, he left me a very, very large sum of money, a house in the Hollow and all of the contents inside, a beat-up Harley that looked like he laid it down on the highway, and a killer black Mustang that was in perfect condition.

At first, I didn't want any of it, and it was not because he wasn't around. Though from the sound of it, he lived a kick-ass life. It was because I felt like it should go to someone he knew. I came to find out later that my mother was the reason for me not seeing him. It was the reason I moved out the day I turned 17.

I ran up the stairs and started to strip my clothes off. When I reached the room, I was in nothing and I threw my dirty laundry into the hamper near my door. I threw my keys on the nightstand and went to the bathroom to take a shower. The bathroom was connected to the bedroom, which was always a bonus when I had girls over. I grabbed a fluffy blue towel from the closet and set it on the sink.

Looking into the mirror, I got a good look at myself for the first time in a long time. I looked like I never saw the sun. I was as white as Casper, and tattoos covered my neck, chest, and arms down to my knucks. My abs were still there and there was more than a hint of muscle on my arms and legs. My hair was short on the sides but long in the front. If I didn't push it up, it would almost cover my eyes.

I flipped open the glass shower door and turned on the water, waiting for it to warm up. As I stepped into the shower, the hot water ran down my body and it washed all the sweat and alcohol from my pours. The water felt so good, but I could feel those pills wearing off, and it was a bummer. I scrubbed up quickly and stepped out, dripping wet as I trailed water to the sink. I grabbed the towel and dried off and headed to the bedroom.

I lit a cig and fell flat on my bed. I blew a big cloud of smoke as I started to daydream about Tes. I couldn't stop thinking about how perfect she was and how much I couldn't wait to text her.

"Shiiittttt." I sat up quickly and looked at my hand. Her name is gone, but her number is still legible. A wave of relief washed over me. I wrote her number down and hit the power button on a black controller lying on my bed. Music from invisible speakers started blasting Pink Floyd's "Wish You Were Here," I laid back down and finished my cig.

I picked up my phone and I added Tes's number. I also noticed I had several text messages and five missed calls.

Going through the texts, I see that one of them is from my man, Brendon. "Hey, what the fuck. Were you at this show? It's insane."

And I have one from this cum dumpster, Meg. "I saw you talking to some fucking tramp. It's actually sad. I told you I wanted to fuck tonight, but I hope you have fun with that slut, faggot."

I laughed when I read that and closed my eyes. It was 12, so I had about 5 hours before I needed to call Tes. I could rest. I faded away fast into my dreams.

CHAPTER 6

<u>The dream</u>

I was lying in my bed when I heard a knock on my bedroom door. I tried to get up, but before I could, the door swung open, and a river of smoke poured in. The doorway was dimly lit just by a single light, and in the doorway stood a silhouette of a woman.

"Who's there?" I whispered.

There was no answer, and the silhouette stepped into the light. It was her; it was the girl that I couldn't get out of my head. It was Tes. I got up, and she walked over to me. She had deep red lipstick, and she was wearing a black sleeveless tank top with "ACDC" written on it with a checkered red and black flannel, a black mini skirt, and black clear socks, which went up right before the knee and those red and black plaid boots with studs on the toes just completed her look. Just watching her was driving me crazy.

She came closer to me.

"Why didn't you call me like you said you were going to?" She asked with a stern yet loving manner.

"I was going to, but I guess I slept too late. I'm sorry."

"I thought you were different," she replied coldly.

"I am. I am different. I'm sorry." I pleaded, moving closer, trying to grab her hand. But she pulled away.

I pushed myself closer to her and tried to grab her hand, but she pulled away.

"I don't think I'm into you anymore," she said, "But I made you this, by the way."

She handed me a giant poster board filled with the most amazing artwork I had ever seen, except the painting; it kept changing. First, it was me and her holding hands with a red heart painted around us. Then, our hands slipped apart, and the heart cracked in two. She disappeared, and I was alone on my knees. It looked like I was crying. Then, I started to age older and older, and I was still alone on my knees. Eventually, I turned into a skeleton, and then the image shifted to a gravestone that read: *"Here lies Michael Wilder, the boy who never became a man.*

The sight of it shocked me, and I stumbled back onto my bed, falling through it and sinking into darkness. The blackness felt endless.

Images of Tes's beautiful face flowed through my mind like Niagara Falls. It was too much to bear. I shot up in a puddle of sweat and breathing super hard, and my heart was pounding out of my chest.

I noticed the time. It was only 5 o'clock.

CHAPTER 7

I took another shower and got dressed. I put on grey sweatpants, a baggy red tattered-up shirt, and my black kicks. I grabbed the keys and my wallet and texted Jimmy as I walked out of the door.

"Yo, what's up fucker? Is my car at your place?

I headed to the Old Reliable and started her up. My phone vibrated, and it was Jimmy.

"What's up, man? Yeah, your piece of shit is here." He replied instantly.

"Sweet man. I'll swing by around 2 am."

"Ight man. I'll be here."

I slammed the car in reverse and started heading down to Auntie's to pick up my mom.

I threw in a tape that I made of *"Cage the Elephant"* and started jamming out.

There ain't no rest for the wicked...

I pulled down the visor and checked myself out in the mirror. While fixing my hair, I noticed a red glow from behind the visor. My heart raced, and I slammed on the brakes as hard as I could. The car came to a screeching halt. Cars honked behind me as I tried to catch my breath. The light turned green, and I slowly let off the brake, accelerating cautiously. I passed the old shutdown movie theater. It still had the title from the last movie that ever played there, some movie called "Gone in 60 Seconds".

I turned the corner and pulled into Auntie's. My mother was standing outside waiting. I was confused. As I pulled up, she got in.

"Why are you outside this early?" I asked.

Her face is in tears.

"What's going on?" I pressed.

She looked at me, but it seemed like she couldn't find the words.

"Mom, what the hell is going on? Did someone hurt you?" I was getting anxious now.

She opened her mouth and began to speak, "I-I-I-I…. I got fired."

"WHAT? HOW?" I was stunned.

"They accused me of stealing tips from other waiters, but I calmly explained that I'd never do that. They didn't believe me and threw me out of the diner." Her cheeks were not completely wet with her tears.

"Did they put their hands on you?" I asked furiously.

"Michael, no."

"Fuck that," I swing my door open and pop the trunk.

"What are you going to do?" she asked, fear in her voice.

"Something I've wanted to do to that fuck since I was 10," I muttered back.

In the trunk, I found a tire iron and some clothes. I moved the clothes out of the way and there it is... I took the bat out.

"Okay, ma. I'll see you later. I love you. Drive safe."

"Mike, please," she begged.

"Na, I'll be fine. Go." I reassured her.

She got in the driver's seat and pulled away. I waited until she left. Thankfully it had been getting darker earlier these days. I snuck around to where the side window was. I noticed a nice family eating and having fun, and it made me think about what I was doing.

But fuck it. I smashed the window. People started screaming, and I took off running with the bat as fast as I could down Franklin Street, heading to Jimmy's.

When I rounded the next corner, I slowed down. I was sweating, and my hair was all messed up. I was out of breath; it made me feel that I was out of shape. As I went closer to my car, I saw it sitting underneath a tree with the windows open. "Fuuucckkk," I muttered. That means bugs could have gotten in.

That Mustang was the most beautiful thing I'd ever owned. I walked past her and headed to Jimmy's door. Music was blasting inside, but all the lights were off.

CHAPTER 8

After about an hour of banging on the door and shouting for Jimmy to open up, I pulled out my thickest credit card and jimmied the door open. As I opened the door, the music blasted even louder and clearer, and weed smoke flowed out like a thick fog. I took off my shoes and set them by the door. Jimmy had that no-shoe policy, and I honestly didn't give a fuck, but if you didn't follow it, he would go on a rant about why it's disgusting. Jimmy's house was nice; he got it after his parents passed away in a car crash. The house had this crazy purple-colored carpet that's soft as fuck when you're tripping.

I heard Jimmy yelling from the other room. I walked into the living room to see Jimmy face down with a girl who was sitting on the black sofa.

"Shit my bad, man. I thought you were just on another bender." I said.

Jimmy laughs as I turn my face away, "It's cool, dude. You want to join?" He asked, barely lifting his head

The girl smiled and said, "Yeah, come on. Jimmy's cock isn't enough."

"HEY, WTF!" Jimmy shouted, laughing

I laughed too, "Na, I'm good. I just came to see what's up for tonight and to pick up my car."

"Well, are you going to go to Cindy's party?" He asked.

"Who the hell is Cindy?" I replied.

Jimmy stopped and sat on the couch, leaned over the wooden coffee table, and cut some lines from the Coke lying on a record. I took a seat on a black-and-white loveseat next to the couch.

The girl walked over to me wearing nothing but a black laced thong. She was pretty hot; she had frizzy hair, and her face was so sexy; her tits were C's on the cusp of being D's. She sat on my lap.

"I'm Cindy, baby," she said, sliding down and undoing the button on my jeans.

I stopped her and looked over to Jimmy. He was doing lines and loving that she was all over me.

"I'm down to go." I said, "Cool if I bring someone?"

"As long as she's fine as hell, baby. It's at my place in the grove off of 21st Street," she said as she walked back over to Jimmy.

I light a joint and lean back.

"I love my fucking life," I muttered.

I stayed at Jimmy's until 10 when I texted Tes, "Hey gorgeous, you wanna go to a party tonight?"

"I'm down. I have to shower and do my makeup. Should take me 10 minutes tops," she replied.

"Do you need a ride from work?" I asked.

"Na. This dude, Antony, is giving me a ride."

Jealousy flared up inside me like a blue flame.

"Is he cute?"

"Yeah. I guess, but he's not my type."

"What is your type?"

"You, silly."

My heart felt whole when she said that.

"Where should I pick you up from?"

"My house. 12 Welsh St. It's the only grey house, I'm sure you remember. Be there around 10:30."

"You got it, beautiful." I texted back.

I threw my phone in my pocket and told Jimmy and Cindy I would see them in a bit.

CHAPTER 9

I headed out, figuring the sooner I got there, the sooner I'd see her face. I was still pretty high and I was my loving life. I hopped in the car and slid back in the leather seat as I started the engine. She purred to life, and I buckled up. Damn, I loved this car. I turned on the radio and bumped some music. The roar of the engine and the music together really got me going. I was only like five minutes away from Tes's place, so I pulled into this place that was just like 711 but a complete rip off. It was called the power hour.

I pulled into a parking space in front of the door and hopped out. Walking into the store, I saw a couple fucking right in the parking lot for everyone to see, fucking nasty. I opened the door and walked in. The smell of cleaning products mixed with the scent of old hotdogs hit my nostrils, and the bright lights blinded me for a second. I scanned around and spotted the chips aisle, fuck yeah. I stood there for about five minutes when I finally decided that I didn't want chips, grabbed a TastyKake, and walked to the counter.

Marcus was working today. I used to go to high school with this guy. Back in the day, he was one crazy motherfucker. I once saw him do a line of a volleyball girl's ass and then fight a cop. Marcus was a tall, lengthy black guy with no hair; he always wore sunglasses to hide the fact that he was high, like 90 percent of the time. I walked up to the counter, and I tossed the TastyKake towards him.

"What's up, man?" I asked.

"Not much, just working. You going to Cindy's party," he replied.

"Hell yeah, are you?" I asked again.

"Nah, man, me and Cindy aren't on the best terms. Last party, I got fucked up on pills, pissed on her bed, and fought her ex because I swore he called me the n-word."

"Hey man, that sounds justified," I laughed.

"But I'll be there," he said, ringing me up and leaned in and whispered, "Yo, I got some shit on me if you want to do some blow."

"Damn, that would be the pick I would need, fuck, I am down, man," I said.

He pulled out a tic tac box filled with the magic white dust, and we both acted like we were dropping Tic Tacs in our mouths and letting it fall into our noses. I snorted hard, and what a fucking head rush. I wouldn't tell anyone to do coke, but damn, it was awesome. I dapped up Marcus and headed out.

I pulled out and headed to Tes's. I was so excited to see her. I was nervous, and I had butterflies in my stomach. I turned down the music as I pulled up to the curve. I sat there fixing my hair and checking my breath. Then, out of nowhere, this cat jumped into my car. What the hell? I couldn't help but laugh as it curled up on my lap. And I pet it; it was actually pretty cute. It's orange and white with black paws and one-half of an ear. It didn't have any tags, though.

I rolled up the windows and got out with the cat. I looked up and saw Tes looking at me from the living room window. I hadn't noticed before, but there was a giant crown painted on the building that said, *"We run this city."* Fucking dope. As I knocked on the door, I could hear footsteps running down the stairs. I heard the door unlock, and that dude who looked like he was a freshman in high school answered the door. He was wearing a colorful rain jacket with a white t-shirt underneath that read *"Fuck It"* in red letters. He had on dark blue pants with ripped along the left side of his leg.

"What's up, man? I'm here to see Tes," I said.

Without a word, he shot back up the stairs, skipping steps as he went.

"I know, man!" He yelled back.

Walking up the stairs, I heard a shit ton of people cheering and fucking going nuts.

I turned the corner and saw Tes doing a row of shots that looked like dark rum but could be whiskey.

She was racing this other dude who looked like he was straight out of a punk rock magazine in the 80s.

She was beating his ass. I started to cheer as she took the last shot. She threw her hands up, and the people in the room went wild. It was crazy. Even with all these people screaming in my ear, I managed to freeze time while looking at Tes. She was so fucking rad. She was wearing this short black dress with horizontal slits that showed off just enough cleavage, and she had got on this burgundy lipstick that melted me. She also had on these black seven-inch heels with clear stems. Time unfroze, and she spotted me.

"Michael!" she screamed as she ran over to me.

"Hey there, beautiful," I said, smiling.

"I'm so glad you came. I honestly missed you so much," she replied.

"I missed you too. How was work?" I asked.

"Shit, it was work. What do you think? She laughed, grabbed my hands, and pulled me closer.

I leaned in for a kiss, and when our lips touched, it was just simply magical, like you know the feeling of your first kiss or like the feeling you get when you're really high, you see that one piece of food that you're craving.

"Follow me," she said, guiding me through the crowd.

"Where are we going," I asked.

"My room, of course, silly," she replied with a smile.

When we got to her room, there was a couple in there going at it.

"Don't worry about them that's just Lizzy and Martha. I let them use the room when they want to get it on," said Tes.

"They don't mind me being here?" I asked, a little taken aback.

"Not at all; we are actually really excited to meet you," Lizzy cuts in.

"Yeah, Tes won't shut up about you. I don't know why; you're just a guy," Martha added, rolling her eyes.

"Martha chill damn," said Tes, "It's nice to meet you."

"What can't shake our hands," Liz smiled.

Lizz and Martha are both naked, and I'd rather not touch two naked girls in front of Tes.

"Yeah, come shake our hands like the gentlemen we've heard about," Lizzy teased.

Lizzy and Martha are lying on the bed naked. Lizzy looks like she could be some type of Spanish. She had long, straight black hair, snake bites, and gauges. Her body was slim, with small perky tits and Hershey kiss nipples. Martha is definitely one of those girls that you wished took cock. Like this girl is bad. She had curly blonde hair and an amazing smile. She was not skinny, though; she was like this, that perfect mixer of thick; her tits were bigger than Lizzy's but smaller than Tes's. I reached out my hand to shake Lizzy's.

"I wouldn't have done that," Tes laughed.

Lizzy grabbed my arm, and Martha grabbed the other. Tes pushed me onto the bed as they pulled, and I landed right in the middle of them. Tes climbed on top, and Lizzy and Martha pinned my arms down.

"He's cute, Tes. I see why you like him," Martha commented.

Tes leaned down and kissed me hard. Then, right above my head, the two other girls leaned over and started making out. Tes leaned up and started a three-way make-out session with the two girls. I'm shocked.

"Wow!" I smiled

They stopped and let me up. My dick is rock-hard.

"You should wipe that drool from your mouth," Lizzy laughed.

"You like that, huh? Maybe one day we can all have some fun together." Tes says, standing up.

There was a knock at the door, and whoever it was didn't sound happy.

"Yo, I saw a guy go in there. What the hell is going on," the deep voice says from the other side of the door.

The girls laughed and opened the door. I was still sitting between Lizzy and Martha while Tes opened the door.

There standing with an angry face is this tall white guy with jet black hair wearing a green day shirt and a pair of light blue jeans. Lizzy and Martha covered themselves with the blanket, but that dude made eye contact.

"Tes, who the hell is this," he asked, glaring.

I stood up. " I'm Michael!"

"I wasn't asking you," he snapped, stepping closer and grabbing Tes's wrist. Her face turned red, and she looked scared..

Fumes flew out of my ears when I saw that, and before I could think, I pushed the blanket off, rushed toward him, and tackled him out of the room, slamming him into the wall. He tried to push me off, but he was unsuccessful.

I brought my right fist back and swung hard, hitting him in the face over and over. With every hit, he sank lower and lower on the wall. The hallway started filling with people, and I heard someone yell, "Damn, he fucked him up!" Tes pulled me off him.

"What the fuck Micheal!?" Tes shouted.

 I was sweating, and my blood was rushing through my veins.

"He grabbed your wrist, and it seems like you were scared," I said, breathless.

"He's my brother; he was just worried."

"Your brother?" I asked, stunned.

"Yeah, I'm here, brother, you psycho," he muttered, rubbing his jaw.

I leaned down, grabbed him, and helped him to his feet.

"I thought you were hurting her, man. I'm sorry," I said, as guilt creeping in.

Everybody went back to parting as I helped him to the bed in the room.

"Tes, I'm so sorry. I was just trying to help,"

"I know, but I can take care of myself, plus you don't need to say sorry to me." She replied.

"At least I know my kid sister will be in good hands." he rubbed his jaw again.

Tes laughed.

"I'm Michael, man," I introduced myself.

"Richie," he replied.

Richie leaned back, and Lizzy kissed his cheek.

"Damn, baby, he did a number on you; shame on you, Micheal."

"I'll be alright." he kissed her back.

"Hey man, you look familiar," I said as I looked at him carefully.

"He's in that band of ages that always plays down at champs,"

"Holy shit, that's fucking dope, man, you guys, sherd."

He dapped me up.

"Thanks, man; we actually have another gig tomorrow at the Stone Pony. You should stop by." He invited.

"No shit, my friend Jessica works there," I replied instantly.

"You are friends with Jessica? I fucked her last year after a show. I was fucking blitzed."

Lizzy smacked him in the back of the head.

"Yeah, she's a little of a band slut, but she's fucking rad."

"No doubt," he laughed.

I looked over at Tes, and she had this half smile on her face.

"Hey, you ready to get out of here and head to the party?" I asked Tes.

"Hell yeah!" She grabbed my hand.

"It was good to meet you all; see you around," I walked out of the door.

Tes shut the door, and I could already hear them going at it. Tes said goodbye to all the randoms at her place, and we headed downstairs to my car.

CHAPTER 10

I opened her car door for Tes, and she smiled warmly at me. The sun had dipped below the horizon, leaving the streets bathing in moonlight, with only one streetlamp illuminating the way. Tes got in the car, still watching me as I closed the door gently behind her.

As I walked around the driver's side, I caught her eyes following me. I went to open my door and noticed the same stray cat again. I picked up the cat and opened the door. As I sat down I set the cat in my lap.

"Is that your cat? He's cute," Tes said, leaning over to pet him.

"He is now. Do you want to hold him?" I asked, lifting the cat from my lap.

"Of course! What are you going to name him?" She asked with a lot of enthusiasm in her voice,

"Jax… Jax would suit him the best!" I smiled and started the car.

We pulled away, heading towards Cindy's, which was just around the corner. When we arrived, we saw a bunch of people gathered outside on the lawn. Laughter and chatter filled the night air.

"Is this it?" Tes giggled, squeezing my hand.

"Yeah, I think so; I've never been here, though," I replied, all while trying to make sense of what was happening on the lawn.

"We could have walked, you know," she teased.

"Yeah, but what if we want to dip out early," I inquired instantly.

"Oh, you wanna dip out early, huh!!" She laughed and nudged me playfully.

"No… Not like that; I mean, if you wanted to, though, I'd be down," I smirked.

"Come on, handsome, let's go inside," she tapped and left the car.

I left the windows down as we exited the car so that Jax would have enough air. The air felt thick as I met Tes on the other side of the car. We locked hands and headed toward the front door. Standing at the foot of the steps was Jimmy, surrounded by two girls and a guy. Jimmy was wearing a pink button-down with dark slim jeans and black vans; as soon as he saw me, he threw up the horns, and I threw them back.

"What's up, man? Who's this?" He said, extending his hand.

"This is Tes. She's fucking rad!!" I said, grinning.

"Hi, it's nice to meet you," said Tes, shaking Jimmy's hand. As they touched, something felt off, weird because it seemed so forced, almost fake.

"Are you ready to get fucked up," I said, brushing the felling aside.

"Hell yeah, man! Let's find Cindy and do some shots," said Jimmy.

He told the trio standing next to him that he'd be right back, and we headed inside. The first inside feels amazing; the air conditioner washed away the nasty humidity from outside. The inside was nice; I could see a lot of black and grey, which gave it a classy vibe. There were a ton of people there that I didn't know. I leaned over

"Yo, you got any blow?" I asked.

"Na! But Cindy might," he replied.

As we made our way upstairs, a girl screamed out Tes's name. Tes turned and spotted her.

"Hold up, guys!" She said, turning to the girl and running down the stairs.

"You guys go ahead. I want to do shots with my friend."

"Alright, I'll be back down in a minute then, beautiful," I called after her with a laugh.

We continue heading up the stairs and make a left at the top. At the end of the hall, there was that red door that was halfway painted black. Strobe lights flash underneath the door. Jimmy opened the door, and a cloud of smoke rolled out. He laughed, and we walked in.

The room was insane; the walls were covered in white fur and black lights. The only furniture was a black and white futon and three zebra-stripped bean bags. The room was just glowing. Inside. Cindy was sprawled across the futon while two others lounged in the bean bags.

"Hey baby, this man is looking for some nose candy," Jimmy said, flopping down onto the futon beside Cindy. She lifted her legs so that Jimmy could sit down and then put her legs back down on top of him

"I have some, but he has to do something for me," she said, smirking.

"Oh yeah? And What would that be?" I said, taking the last remaining bean bag.

"This party is lacking in entertainment; I need you to sing for us," she giggled.

"I can't sing," I protested, rubbing my head. Jimmy laughed, and Cindy sat up, her eyes gleaming.

"That's not what I heard. I heard you get your talent from your real father," she replied.

"How do you know about my father?" I started to get a little agitated as if a flicker of irritation had risen in my chest.

She stood and started to move toward me, trying to sit on my lap, but I stopped her.

"I got a girl here," I said with a somber tone.

"It's okay, baby. I know you here with Tes," she replied while throwing her finger towards me.

"How do you know all of this?" I asked, sitting up in the bean bag, my suspicion growing.

Cindy's face turned serious for a moment, her playful demeanor fading.

"You really haven't heard of me before," she asked with a straight face.

Jimmy's face went pale, a stark contrast to his earlier energy.

"You know what? I'll explain later… Right now, you sing or no blow," she said, dangling a bag of nose candy in front of me.

"Fuck it," I said with a shrug. "Where do you want me to sing? And I'm gonna need a guitar." I stood up, laughing.

CHAPTER 11

I followed Cindy downstairs where the party was full alive. The energy was electric. As I glanced into the kitchen, I spotted Tes talking to a group of people, and a strange feeling washed over me—it seemed like she had been here before. I could feel the high wearing off, and paranoia started creeping in.

When we entered the living room, there was a microphone against the wall. Cindy pulled it out and hooked the amp and the microphone. The room hummed with anticipation.

"Yo, did you tell Cindy about me?" I whispered to Jimmy, my voice laced with unease.

"You'll know what's going on soon," he said, giving my back a reassuring pat.

Cindy tapped the mic, her voice cutting through the noise. "Listen up, you degenerates! I've got a little surprise for you motherfuckers tonight!"

The crowd roared and gathered around. I saw Tes coming into the living room. My nerves started acting up, sending goosebumps across my skin.

"Micheal, get your ass up here!" Cindy called out, laughing

Reluctantly, I stepped forward as she handed me a guitar.

"The guy right here is Martin Wilder's son, and he's about to rock your fucking world!" Cindy shouted away on the microphone.

Panic rose inside me. I didn't even know what I was going to play, and internally, I was freaking out.

I strummed the guitar and cleared my throat, "How's everyone doing tonight?" There was nervousness in my voice.

The crowd cheered, their energy giving me a small boost.

"I'm only doing this for a bag of blow, but I'll do my best," I joked. The crowd laughed, and I saw Tes smiling at me; a surge of confidence hit me like a wave.

"This is a song I wrote when I was coming down from a 10-day bender. Hope you enjoy it."

I started out by playing a taste rift and I closed my eyes and began to sing.

One, I don't belong here

Two, I gotta get out of here

And three, I feel so lonely, and I don't know where I am

Please help me. I need your help. I'm lost, and I can't find my way out

I need to scream; I need to shout no way out

No way out!

I see the light at the end of the tunnel

I'm tripping and falling

Stumbling and crawling

I need an angel to hear my call

I need a hand to get me through this hall

Hear my words and feel my faith

I don't belong here. My life's at stake

All I feel is hate

But then I feel a warm glow

And there I go

I'm home

When I opened my eyes, the room had erupted into chaos. People were going wild, the sound of applause and cheers filling the air.

"Thank you. Have a good night, guys!" I said, setting down the guitar and walking over to Cindy

The crowd was asking for another song, but I was done for the night.

"I believe you owe me a bag of blow," I smiled.

Cindy tossed me the bag with a smirk.

"I knew you could do it," she said, bumping into me playfully.

Tes ran up, hugged me, and kissed my cheek.

"Oh my God! That was amazing!" Tes said with a huge smile on her face.

"Thank you, beautiful. Do you wanna go do some lines?" I asked with a smile

"Of course," she said as we followed Cindy back upstairs.

CHAPTER 12

Upstairs, I dumped the whole bag onto the glass coffee table Cindy had dragged in from the hallway. Jimmy handed me a razor blade, and I cut four lines. The white powder gleamed under the black light as everyone settled in. I sank into one of the bean bags, and Tes took the one next to me. Jimmy found a spot on the couch with Cindy perched on his lap. I couldn't help but notice Cindy's neon orange lipstick as she pressed play on a remote control. Queen's News of the World began to play softly, one of my favorite albums.

"Cindy, how did you know those things about me? And how did you know I brought Tes?" I asked, putting the razor blade down and looking up at her.

Cindy smirked.

"I'm only going to answer one of those questions today. I'll let you choose which one it is, baby," Cindy kissed Jimmy on the cheek, leaving glowing orange lipstick in the shape of her lips.

I had really wanted to know both, and I was having a hard time choosing. Tes grabbed my hand, and when I looked at her, she smiled. I felt this warmth, and I knew what I wanted Cindy to answer then.

I pulled a dollar from my pocket, rolled it up, and snorted the first line. A wave of euphoria rushed over me, and self-confidence surged through my body.

"You're going to tell me the truth and not some bullshit, right?" I said as my nose started to bleed like a waterfall.

Tes noticed and handed me a tissue from her purse. I wiped the blood off my lip and shoved the tissue into my nose.

"Of course" she said, as she smiled at Tes.

Without further hesitation, I said, "Tell me how you know all that stuff about me."

Cindy lit a blunt from her purse, exhaling a thick cloud of smoke, "Your father, Martin Wilder, use to jam with my dad, and he occasionally bought coke and weed off me when I started selling," she passed the blunt to Jimmy and continued, "Martin was an amazing man; he had the voice of god and the guitar skills unlike any man. He loved you; he'd show us pictures and tell stories your mom told him about your musical skill..."

"That can't be true. Stop lying. My father was a great man, but he never loved me," I interrupted, my voice bitter.

"If you interrupt me again, I'll cut off your dick, you hear?" Her face turned serious.

"Understood, continue," I said as Tes bent down and snorted the second line.

"Like I was saying, he had skill, but your mother wouldn't let you see him. She thought he might be a terrible influence on you and you might end up like him. We can see how well that turned out," She laughed as Jimmy passed the blunt back to her.

I tried to process everything, but I was flying high, so all I could muster was, "Wow, did your dad play in the band?"

"Yeah, he was the drummer… Haden star." She replied.

"You're Haden Star's daughter? Holy shit! Do you follow in your father's footsteps? I laughed.

"Yeah, I'm legendary," she said, grinning. Jimmy tapped her arm, and she moved off his lap.

"We should jam sometime; we could be an amazing team," I said to her.

Cindy laughed, then leaned down and snorted the third line. I could see that euphoric glow wash over her face. "We'd need a bass player first, but I'm down," she said before kissing Jimmy. They started going at it on the couch, Jimmy on top of her, kissing her neck.

I glanced at Tes. She was biting her lip, clearly in the mood. I leaned over and kissed her, and she kissed me back. As I leaned further in, she slowly laid down on the floor. I kissed every inch of her body, my excitement building with each moan from Cindy.

When I reached the end of Tes's skirt and lifted it past her hips, I realized she wasn't wearing any underwear. I looked up and smiled, but before I could do anything, Tes grabbed my head and shoved it down. Just as I was about to lick, there was a knock at the door.

Cindy yells out, almost moaning the words

"Go away, mother fucker!!" Cindy yelled in a voice thick with frustration.

I go to eat her out again, but the knock grows louder.

"Fuck!" Cindy yelled as she got up, and Jimmy wiped his mouth. I sat up as Tes adjusted her dress.

"What the fuccc…..." Cindy swung the door open.

Standing in the doorway was a very tall, muscular man wearing a black hoodie, blue jeans, and black kicks. A tattoo above his left eyebrow read **GRIM** in bold red letters.

"Oh shit, I didn't know you were going to be here tonight," Cindy said, her voice suddenly filled with fear.

He looked angry as he looked over at Tes. He walked in and I stood up to my feet as he walked closer to me and Tes.

He walks even closer to Tes, but I get in the middle of them.

As he got closer, Jimmy whispered, "Yo, get the fuck out of his way, Michael."

"FUCK THAT! CAN I HELP YOU?" I practically spat the words in his face.

"Michael, stop," Tes said from behind me.

"Yeah, listen to the whore before you end up in an unmarked grave," the man sneered, now face to face with me. He reeked of sweat and something worse.

"Nah, FUCK THAT! WHAT'S UP PUSSY?" I yelled.

The man grabbed me by the shirt, lifting me off the ground. "You little piece of shit," he growled.

I smashed my face into his, he let me go and stumbled back.

"Michael, no! Stop! You don't know what you're doing!" Tes cried.

I charged at him, slamming us both into the wall. I felt invincible. He punched me in the gut, but I barely felt it. I landed a couple of punches to his face, sending him to the floor.

"Fucking nerd," I spat, looking down at him.

The man rolled over, pulled out a black 9mm, and aimed it at me as he used the wall to get back on his feet.

"Everyone downstairs. Now," he barked, striking me with the gun as I passed. I fell to my knees, but Tes was quick to help me up.

CHAPTER 13

I held my head as I walked down the stairs. The music was pounding, and people were still partying. My head throbbed with each step, and as we reached the bottom, everyone turned to stare at us.

"Everyone get the fuck out! Now!" The tattooed man yelled, firing a shot into the ceiling

Everyone screamed and scattered in every direction. A couple of people trip over each other as they stumble out of the house. I clutched my head as the man led us to the couch. We all sat down; Tes sat next to me and placed her hands gently on my face to check on my head.

"Are you alright?" Tes asked, wiping a bit of blood from the back of my head.

"I'm fine," I groaned, my pride hurt more than anything else.

The man, still pointing the gun at us, walked over to the laptop, blasting music, and shut it off.

"Do you know who I am?" He asked calmly.

"You're Mr. Keith, aka *Alpha*," Cindy said, her voice shaky with fear.

"That's right, Cindy… And who do I work for?" He chuckled. That laughter increased the nervousness in the room.

"You work for my goddess faith," Cindy replied, still afraid.

"I've come here to collect the debt you owe Faith, but right now, I just want to kill this fucking prick," he said, pointing the gun at me.

The fucking coke was wearing off, and all my confidence faded quickly.

"Look, man, I'm sorry; I was just trying to protect my friends," I said to him, still holding my head, which was now aching.

"I don't give a fuck what you were trying to do," he snapped, walking closer to me.

I should have kept my fucking mouth shut. He pressed the black cold steel barrel of his 9mm against my forehead.

"No, please!!" Tes desperately screamed, standing up.

Keith shoved her back down to her knees, and in all this action, the gun slightly slipped off my forehead, and a slow-motion moment kicked in. I realized I had two choices: sit there and let him blow my brains out or try to grab the gun and risk getting one of my friends hurt.

Like a coward coming down hard from a high, I chose the first option. Time resumes and the 9mm was again pressed back against my forehead.

"Come on, man, please," I begged with my hands down at my side.

Everyone around us was screaming. Keith's grip tightened, and his trigger finger slowly pulled back.

"I hope you have fun in hell, kid," he said. Just then, the front door swung open, and standing there was a 5'3" Asian woman.

CHAPTER 14

Keith quickly pulled the gun away from my forehead and spun around. Faith walked face to face with him and slapped him, leaving a tiny red handprint hand across his face.

"I told you to collect the money, not carry out an execution," she snapped.

Keith lifted his free hand to his face. "I'm sorry, it won't happen again."

He stepped aside, and she moved closer to me. She wore a light blue embroidered jean jacket, a white T-shirt, and black jeans. She leaned in, grabbed my face, and glared.

"So, who the fuck do you think you are!!" she screamingly asked.

I started to answer, but she interrupted me, "That was a Rhetorical question, sweety."

She scratched my face as she walked toward Cindy.

Tes grabbed my hand tightly, and I whispered to her, "It's going to be alright."

Faith stopped in front of Cindy and smiled. She leaned over, and I noticed Cindy couldn't help staring at her cleavage.

"Nothing wrong with that," I thought to myself.

"You have caused me a lot of grief my little sub," she said, as she grabbed her chin.

"I'm sorry, my mistress…" Cindy replied, lifting her head and trying to kiss Faith.

Faith pushed Cindy back down softly.

"Where's my money, honey?" Faith asked.

Cindy pointed to the front door, "It's outside," she said nervously.

Faith smirked.

"May I get up and show you, my goddess?" Cindy asked, smiling.

Faith waved her hand upward, showing her approval. And Cindy stood up and walked over to the front door. She knelt down near the framing of the door and pushed the white door trimmings to the side. Sitting in the cubby hole is a large wad of money.

"Damn, babe, I didn't know that was there!" Jimmy laughed.

Keith shot Jimmy a dirty look as Cindy pulled out the cash and tossed it to Faith.

"Is it all here?" Faith asked with a wink.

"Not exactly. There's 500 missing," Cindy replied nervously.

Faith walked over to the glass coffee table in the middle of the room, grabbed an ashtray, and threw it at the table, shattering the glass.

"Fuck Faith! That table was expensive!" Cindy screamed.

Faith walked over to the wall and pulled out a knife from her boot.

"Faith, please! I'll get it to you, baby," Cindy begged.

Faith stuck the knife in the wall and walked toward us, gauging a hole in the wall all the way. She puts the knife to Cindy's throat.

"I need like a week, and I promise I'll get it…" Cindy begged again.

Faith stayed silent, softly pressing the knife against Cindy's neck.

"What did I tell you when you were asked to work for me?" Faith grinned.

"You told me you'd never give me any slack just because you know me," Cindy whispered.

"I kno..." Cindy continued in a shaky voice.

Before she could finish, Faith grabbed Cindy's hair, yanked it back, and pressed the knife harder against her skin.

"That's enough!!" I screamed.

Faith turned to me and walked closer.

"What makes you think I won't cut your throat, pretty boy," she sneered.

"Because I'm gonna pay you what she owes and more," I said, standing firm.

"Oh! Are you?" She mocked.

I reached back for my wallet, and Keith immediately pointed the gun at me again.

"God damn! I'm just getting my wallet," I said in a frustrated tone.

I grabbed out my wallet and pulled out the money I had.

"Here's 700 bucks now; please leave!" There was an assertion in my tone.

Faith took the money and slapped me hard. "I'm not a damn joke. I'll see you around, Cindy."

Kieth butted the gun away, and the two of them walked out of the house.

"Let's get out of here, Tes," I said, taking her hand. We headed for the door. Cindy stood up.

"Thank you, I owe you," she said quietly.

"Don't mention it," I replied without looking back.

We got in the car and I started driving toward the house.

"I'm so sorry you had to go through that," I said in an embarrassing tone.

"It was scary, but I'm okay. Thank you for being so tough," she replied, smiling softly.

I smiled and just kept driving.

CHAPTER 15

I woke up to the sun in my eyes and Tes laying on my chest. God, that felt so right. There was no place I'd rather have been at that moment. I just lay there looking at the ceiling, knowing that nothing that day could be better than that moment. Her warm breath on my bare chest made me smile. All good times had to come to an end, unfortunately. From across the room, the song "Role Models" by J. Cole started to play—it must have been Tes's phone. She groaned as she woke up. I let out a small laugh.

"Good morning, beautiful," I said.

She dug her head into me as the phone stopped ringing. I was thankful that she ignored it. The smell of perfume and weed still lingered in the air, just like the first time I was in her room. J. Cole started again; Tes rolled off of me. The blanket slipped down from her nips, and I immediately got a stiffy.

"Whoever is calling is dead to me," she joked with a smile.

She got out of bed, wearing nothing but red lace panties. Her hair flowed down her back, glistening in the sunlight. Tes bent down and picked up her purse, rummaging through it until she found her phone. I reached over and grabbed a pack of smokes, lighting one as she answered the call. The sun hit the cloud of smoke I exhaled just right.

"Hey, what's up, J"

J? jimmy? But that didn't sound like him.

"Nah, you told me I'm off today," she continued. Definitely not Jimmy.

"Oh, that can't be Jimmy," I thought to myself again.

I ashed my cig in the skull ashtray nearby.

"Come on, I'm with Michael," she said.

I smiled at her, but she was not looking.

"Yes, that Michael, I'm not coming in. I gotta go bye," she said, tossing her phone aside before crawling back onto the bed.

"Let me get one of those, please," she asked.

"Sure thing!" I light the cig in my mouth and hand it to her.

"So, who was that, your boss?" I asked, exhaling the smoke.

"Yeah, one of them," she said, taking a drag.

At that moment, she reminded me of one of those girls in the magazines.

"Sounds like they wanted you to work," I said.

"Yeah, but fuck them. I want to spend time with you," she replied with a broad smile on her face.

She ashed on a towel near the bed, and I couldn't help but wonder about her a bit.

"What do you want to do today, then?" I asked.

"Let's go to your place!" she rubbed my leg.

I finished my cig and put it out in the ashtray.

"Yeah, I gotta get changed anyway. Do you wanna shower?" I asked her.

"Nah, I can do that at your place!" She replied with a wink.

I smiled as I got up. "*Damn, I gotta piss,*" feeling an urgent need to hit the bathroom.

"Hey, where's the bathroom again?" I asked.

"It's right outside the room, to the left," she replied.

I slipped on my clothes from yesterday and walked out toward the bathroom. Two closed doors sat in front of me, one on the left and one on the right.

"Fuck! She didn't tell me which side,"

I chose the door on the left. I knocked and didn't hear anything. I opened the door, and sitting on the toilet was the dude who was passed out underneath the coffee table.

"Oh shit, man, my bad!" I closed the door.

"All good, bro!" I heard from behind the door.

My mouth felt dry, and I was exhausted. I needed water, so I headed down the narrow hallway toward the kitchen.

The apartment was a mess, reeking like a frat house, with clothes and wrappers everywhere. The carpet was so stained it looked like a Jackson Pollock painting. In the living room, a couple was passed out, buck naked on the couch. The light hit them just right. The dude had a defined body, like a CrossFit enthusiast, and the girl looked like someone had taken their time creating her. It gave me an idea for an album cover. As I passed, they started to wake up, and I tried hard not to make a sound.

"Hey babe, can you get me water from the fridge?" The guy groaned.

The woman huffed, "Fine!"

I turned on the faucet and reached for one of the glasses sitting on a green rag near the sink. As I filled it, some water dripped down. The cold water on my hands felt so good.

"Damn, I need a shower," I thought to myself.

As I turned off the faucet, I heard the fridge open behind me.

"I wouldn't drink that water, dude," she said.

I turned around to see that naked girl bent over in the fridge. The light must be following her because the way it bounces off her ass was insane.

"I appreciate the heads up," I dumped the water down the sink.

"Here, catch!!"

She tossed me a bottle of water. I spun around just in time to catch it, immediately looking away from her.

"Thanks, I'm thirsty as fuck," I said.

She laughed and walked closer, reaching out.

"Hey, can you move over? I just have to grab something from behind you," she said.

"Yeah, my bad!" I laughed

I cracked open the bottle of water as she opened a drawer. The water felt like heaven on my dry lips, and I finished the whole thing in seconds.

"Damn, dude, you good??" She said, taking out three J's from the drawer.

"I feel like shit; you know you are naked, right!" I laughed.

She closed the door and looked at me, lighting one of the three joints. She blew smoke in my face as she stepped closer. She was so close that if I moved, I would have brushed up against her nipples. She lifted my hand and placed the joint in it.

"I'm just fucking with you, man. Enjoy. Tes rolled it. She's got good hands."

From the living room, I heard the guy, "Babe stops fucking with him; I need that water."

She laughed and headed to the couch.

"Fuck man, this is a madhouse." I thought to myself.

I took a deep puff and tossed the water bottle in the recycling bin. As I headed back to Tes's room, I overheard her on the phone.

"Yeah, man, I know, but this isn't fair… Yeah, but why? Fuck, fine!" I opened the door just as she hung up the phone.

She was all dressed at this point. She was wearing a green sweater with a Slytherin logo on it, dark blue high-watered pants, and black and white vans. Her hair was in a messy ponytail.

"Damn, I'm a Ravenclaw," I thought.

"Hey, what's goin' on?" I asked.

"I have to go to work. Can you drop me off at the store?" she sighed.

"Yeah, no problem, beautiful. Do you want to stop to get breakfast?" I offered.

"No, I have to get there quickly," she giggled.

I slipped on my shoes, and we headed out of her room. Tiger was in the kitchen making something on the stove. Ted and Macy were still on the couch; I tried not to look their way. I didn't want Tes to see me looking at a naked girl.

Tes laughed. "Damn, Macy! Looking good, girl."

Ted slapped Macy's ass, and Macy slapped him playfully in the face.

"Where are you off in my sweater?" Macy laughed.

Oh, so it wasn't even hers. There was still hope.

"Asshat Jimmy wants me to come into work today," Tes laughed.

I tossed a peace sign as we headed downstairs to my car. Just as we stepped outside, the clouds covered the sun, and a cold wind made me wish I'd brought my jacket. I lit a cig as I started the engine. Coldplay blasted on the radio, and as I reached to turn it down, I burncd my hand with the cig.

"Fuck!" I wince and put the cig in my mouth.

Tes grabbed my hand and blew slightly on the burn as she pulled an ointment out of her purse. It was a plain white tube with no labels.

"Hey, what is th…" as I was asking, the ointment instantly soothed my skin

"It's a special ointment I made. It feels better, right?" Her tone was concerning.

 "Yeah! Almost instantly," I smiled back at her.

I puffed a big cloud and flicked the cig out the window as we headed down the road.

"So, what's in that ointment?" I asked.

"It's a secret cutie…" She smirked.

"Of course," I laughed, turning up the music.

We finally pulled up to Monic's, and Tes hopped out in a rush, not waiting for me to come to a full stop.

"Call me later, okay?" She called back, already halfway to the door.

Before I could say, of course, she was already halfway into work. I lighted another cig and called Jimmy.

Ring… ring … ring…

"Hey, this is Jimmy; you know what to do…"

"Fuck I got his voicemail. I'll just go home," I thought to myself.

I hung up, popped a K-turn, and headed for the exit. Right when I was about to turn left, I saw Tes's purse—black and purple with the logo branded all over it. I threw the car in reverse and backed up until I was at the store again. I grabbed the purse and opened the car door. Her purse was heavier than it looked. I got out and closed the door. I could smell the rain that was about to start. On my way to the door, I noticed small wet spots on the ground starting to appear; luckily, I made it to the door before it started to pour. When I stepped foot into Monic's, I realized that I'd never actually been in this store before. It was cold, and the lights were dim. There was faint music playing in the background, and the clothes looked like a weird combo of old and young women. Scanning for Tes, I noticed a woman assisting another woman.

"Excuse me, miss," I said, raising my hand and walking over.

"How can I help you, sir?" She grinned.

"Hey, I dropped off Tes, and she left her purse in my car," I lifted the purse.

The woman looked at me and gave me a look that a dog gives when it's confused.

"She's not working today; she has off," she said, turning back to the other customer.

What the fuck! I headed back to my car. It was still pouring, so I ran and jumped inside. I fixed my hair and turned the car over, and she purred loudly.

I picked up my phone and called Tes.

Ring... ring... ring...

The phone went to voicemail, and I hung up and shot her a text.

"Hey, you left your purse in the car. Guess I'll give it to you when you get off."

I headed back to my house. On the way, I passed by Jimmy's to see if he was home. The rain was coming down so hard and so fast I could barely see the road. Cars were blasting by me as I threw my blinker on to turn left onto Jimmy's street. The final car passed, and I headed onto his street. Jimmy's house had an overhang that covered a good portion of his driveway, and right out in front, I saw Jimmy, Cindy, and someone else I couldn't quite make out. I pulled up to the curb and hopped out, the car still on.

"Yo, Jimmy!" I yelled as I ran under the overhang of the house.

"Oh Shit Micheal!" Jimmy said as if he was caught by a surprise.

"Hey Cindy, what's up, girl," I waved at her.

Cindy said nothing back to me, almost looking very unhappy that I showed up. The other person still had their back towards me, so I couldn't see who it was.

"What are you fuckers up to!!" I laughed, lighting a cig.

The air felt stiff, and I really felt unwanted.

"We are just chillin', talking shop," Jimmy handed a blunt over to Cindy.

"Hey baby, can you come back later?" Cindy got up and smiled, putting the blunt between my lips and tapping my ass.

"Yeah, man, no problem!" I said while taking a puff, and then I ran back to my car.

I hopped in my car and stared at the mystery person. "Fuck it's probably just some low-level dealer Jimmy's selling to the wholesale." I thought to myself. I slammed the car on the driver and smashed the gas.

The water made my tires slip better, and I did a burnout all the way down the street.

Bing. Text from jimmy

"Asshole."

I smiled as I pulled onto my street and pulled into my driveway.

CHAPTER 16

Six Hours Later…

The TV light illuminated the room as I sat there playing on my phone. I had textcd Tcs about something, but there was no answer. I wondered where she had gone after I dropped her off and why she felt the need to lie about it. The thought of going through her purse crossed my mind earlier, but I wasn't that type of person. I figured she would text me when she needed it.

Bing. It's a text from Marcus.

The text read, "Hey man, wyd?"

"Just watching toons and about to roll up; why?" I replied.

"There's this poker game going on tonight. You down?" he responded back.

"I don't know how to play poker, man," I laughed.

"It's simple. Just match the cards, I think," he replied back.

I paused for a minute and thought about it.

"Why do you want me to come so badly?"

"Okay, so there's this dime that's going, and I want her bad man."

"Hound dog, lol."

"I need your help distracting her friend and backing me up if I get into some shit."

I thought back to yesterday when he shared that coke with me. Damn, I kind of owed him.

"Okay, man, fine. What time? How much money should I bring?"

"SSIICCKK!!, I'll shoot you the details."

Forwarded text from Marcus

"Marcus, the place is called the Snaps house. The address is 6 Nuttin Way by the water. Be there at 8 pm; buy-in is $200 max buy $2000. The game is 2 / 5 NLH. Hope you know how to play".

I switched the light on and located some threads. I chose a more laid-back look: dark blue jeans that had that dirty work vibe, a white T-shirt with a small M logo on the chest, black and white Vans, and a brown fuzzy winter hat. I grabbed my wallet and $300 cash from my top drawer. It was now 5 PM, so I had three hours until I could potentially lose my money. I threw on my black leather jacket and headed out the door. It wasn't raining anymore, but it sure smelled like the storm had yet to finish. I grabbed an umbrella from my trunk and tossed it in the back seat. I hopped in, and before I started the car, I lit a cig.

"Man, I need to quit these things," I thought to myself.

I started the car and decided just to drop off Tes's purse at her place. That way, I didn't have to worry about it anymore. Plus, her place was not too far from the game tonight.

I parked out front and turned off the car. Grabbing the purse, I got out and shut the door on my way to the front porch.

Knock… Knock… Knock

I heard footsteps and the sound of rustling before the door finally opened; it was Ted. He had on cartoon pajama bottoms and no shirt, and he was in a red robe. Looked like he'd already been partying.

"Mike!!" He said, all raspy.

"What's up, Ted! I'm just dropping off Tes's purse, mind if I drop it in her room?"

"Mike, I wouldn't want it any other way," he smiled.

As Ted stumbled and tripped back up the now-dirty brown carpeted stairs, I followed closely behind. When we reached the top, I saw that the place had been cleaned from top to bottom. The smell of warm apples filled the air, and the sound of a vacuum mixed with Elton John's music flooded my ears.

"Ted, what's the special occasion?" I smirked.

"Uh?" He looked at me, confused.

"Why are you guys cleaning," I continued asking.

Ted sat down and put his feet up on the glass coffee table.

"Oh, that's Victoria. She cleans when she has off. Honestly, she's the only one who does," he replied.

I walked to Tes's room and opened the door. The room was spotless—no clothes on the floor, and it didn't smell like before. The carpet was different from the rest of the apartment; it was a burgundy color, making the art on the wall really pop. I tossed her bag on the freshly made bed and turned around to see a beautiful plus-sized woman standing in the doorway. She had curves for days. She had brown hair, brown eyes, and a Jack Skellington tattoo on her left forearm. She was wearing a black bandana tied backward on her head, a white tank top, and a pair of blue high-waisted pants.

"Hey, who are you, and why are you in Tes's room? TTEEEEDDDYYY!!!!! Why do you invite these people over,"

I could hear Ted murmur, "Don't call me that, Vic."

"Actually, I'm Micheal, Tes's… friend/fling."

"And that gives you the right to come into her room with no one here?"

"I was just dropping off her purse; she left it in my car this morning."

I pointed to the purse. She walked right next to me and grabbed the purse.

"I just cleaned in here; you can at least hang it up. I'm Victoria, by the way."

She hung the purse up and reached her hand out to shake mine. I met her halfway and shook her hand.

"It's a pleasure to meet you," I smiled.

Her hands were soft and the way she was looking at me was getting me all worked up.

"Likewise," she leaned towards me and whispered in my ear, sending chills throughout my body.

I brushed by her, my boner grazing her leg. I could have sworn I saw her smile.

Heading back to the living room, Ted was lying on the couch smoking a blunt, blowing smoke rings as he itched his balls.

"Hey, you wanna tok," he gestured the blunt my way.

I took a minute and thought about it.

Fuck it!

"Hell, yeah, man!" I said.

I sat down next to his feet, grabbed the blunt from him, and leaned back.

I took a big pull and slowly let it out, and began coughing uncontrollably, Ted laughed and sat up.

"Gotta cough to get off," he slapped my back and took the smoke back.

I started to laugh, and the coughing subsided.

"That's some good shit," I said as I looked over at him.

Vic walked into the room and headed toward Ted.

"Let me get a hit," she said, reaching out for the weed. Ted gladly passed it to her, and she took a seat next to me.

She took a big pull and passed it back to me.

"So, you are into Tes?" Ted said while he was grinding more weed.

"She's unique," I barely got it out as I exhaled a cloud.

I passed the blunt, and Vic was looking at Ted in a weird way like they knew something that I didn't.

"Where is she anyway? She's usually home today," Vic said.

"I dropped her at work today, somebody named J called her in," I responded back in a sober tone.

"J, oh shit, man, she tricked you into dropping her off at that guy's house," Ted laughed.

"Ted shut up; it's cool that you did that for her."

"Yeah, I actually dropped her off at Monics, who is J," I say intrigued

Ted and Vic break out into a huge laugher

"Honey, she ditched you to go to her other job because she's ashamed," Vic said, calming down.

"Oh, what's her other job?"

"She's a…." Ted began to speak but was interrupted by Vic when she threw a pillow at his face.

"She should tell you that, not us. Aight that right, Ted?" said Vic.

"First, don't throw shit at me, second, yeah! She should be the one."

I laughed it off and stood up.

"Alright! I gotta bounce; thanks for the sweet," I dapped up Ted and Vic and headed toward the door.

"Btw don't think I didn't notice you looking at Macey this morning. She's fine as hell, right!?" Ted said Jokingly.

I laughed it off and headed down the stairs and out to my car.

I still had about two hours to kill, so I decided to nap in my car. I turned on the radio and put the air on. I put the seat all the way back, leaned it back as far as it could go, and passed out.

CHAPTER 17

BUZZ BUZZ BUZZ

I snapped awake, eyes still shut. Grabbing my phone from the cup holder and fumbling it a couple of times before finally sitting up. I looked at the phone; there were three missed calls from Marcus and two new texts, one from Mom and the other from Tes.

I wiped my sweaty face with a rag I had lying in the back. Checking the time, I had about fifteen minutes before I needed to be at the poker game, just five minutes down the street. So, I lit a cigarette and pulled off, eyes still half-closed as I opened the text from my mom while I was driving.

"Hey, sweetie, we want you to come for dinner tomorrow night around 6-ish. Okay, okay, I love you. ~Love Mom."

As I went to reply, headlights suddenly flashed in my eyes. Horns blared as I swerved quickly, narrowly avoiding a black SUV speeding past with the horn still blaring.

"Fuck that was close!!!!"

I put my phone down as I reached the house, I parallelly parked between Marcus's BMW and a White Ford Explorer.

I double-checked that I had my money and went out, locking my doors behind me.

I lit a cigarette and headed toward the door that first dragged reassuring me that I'll be okay. I saw a very beautiful woman talking to Marcus. She was wearing a pink lace dress adorned with a rose pattern and matching pink heels. She turned and walked inside as I reached the front steps.

"Marcus, who was that?" I asked, a small escaping me.

"Just a friend, I'll introduce you later. Come on! The game is about to start."

We made our way through the small crowd, moving from one room to another until we finally reached a back room with only four people sitting at a slightly large poker table. I immediately recognized, there was a man in the corner of the room behind a table with chips.

I approached him, and as I did, I noticed the other players at the table eyeing me up.

Handing him the money I brought; I tried to sound casual.

"Nice weather we're having today," I said with a casual smile.

The man smirked as he handed me a rack of chips of two different colors, red and green.

I turned and headed toward the table where Marcus was grabbing his chips.

"Seems like we meet again, Mr. Bond," the woman from the other night said, her eyes narrowing as she smirked at me.

"Pleasure to see you again," I responded, sitting down and getting comfortable.

I unpacked my chips and make two stacks; one of red and one of green.

"You know this guy?" a man in a burgundy hoodie asked, his ridiculous shades making him look even dumber.

"Bright in here, huh!" I said shyly.

"Yes, but don't worry, you're still my favorite deer," she said, winking at me.

The other two men were glued to their phones, clearly disinterested. Marcus took his seat, and the dealer stepped up to the table.

"I have to admit, Faith, I'm not familiar with this game, but I'm excited nonetheless."

"No worries," Faith replied, grinning, "I'll be happy to take your money."

The dealer cut the deck and dealt two cards to each player.

"The game is no-limit. Texas Hold'em blinds are 2/5," the dealer announced, "Just a friendly game."

∴ *(2/5 means $2 small blind & $5 big blind)*

As I looked at my cards, I tried not to give away any tells; I have watched a lot of poker videos but have never really played myself before. The night went pretty well, I lost some, and I won some, and eventually, I was up at $2000. Marcus went broke, and the other guys had few small stacks remaining compared to me and Faith.

The dealer gave out the cards, and my cards showed *King of Hearts and King of Spades. That's gotta be good,* I chuckled to myself, feeling a bit too confident.

Everyone folds except Faith. She just called.

The dealer burned a card and dealt the flop: Queen of diamonds, King of diamonds, Eight of spades.

When I saw the *King of Diamonds*, my heart started to pump as fast as it could. I was the first to act, and I checked.

"Bet 30," Faith said, tossing in the chips.

I hesitated for a moment, trying to keep my poker face in place.

"Call."

I heard Marcus talking to the guy in the burgundy hoodie about his day at work, glancing my way like he was trying to figure me out. I gave him a quick look as if to say, "Do you mind?" He stopped talking, sensing the tension. The dealer burned a card and dealt the turn: Eight of diamonds.

I looked at Faith. Now, I had a full house, and I was hoping she would bet big.

"Your friend owes me a lot of money," she said, eyeing me. "Are you gonna be the same as her? Bet 100."

She tossed the chips into the middle, rolling all over the green velvet table.

"Since you bring that up, how much does she owe you?" I asked, trying to sound nonchalant.

"Call."

I tossed the chips in, and the dealer burned a new card over the table.

Faith stopped him before he dealt the card.

"She owes me 15 grand. She is not too smart with her money."

The other players, who had been casually scrolling through their phones, were now glued to the conversation.

"Is that all?" I laughed.

"And you smashed up her living room and ruined a party for that chub change? You must be desperate." My laughter was cut short by her anger.

Faith slammed her fist on the table, startling everyone, including me.

"Mike, Mike, Mike…" She said, leaning forward. "What makes you think you can come into my poker game and talk to me with such disrespect?"

"I just meant a woman of your stature shouldn't be worried about such things, right?"

I felt a presence behind me, and when I glanced at the mirror on the wall, I saw the man who had handed me the chips earlier now standing behind me.

"How about this then, Micheal," Faith said, her voice dripping with venom. "If you win this hand, I'll erase the debt, but if not, then you both owe me 15 grand, and you have to let my friend behind you fuck your ass on camera."

My stomach dropped. Money is one thing, but I sure as hell wasn't going to let some dude fuck me.

I quickly countered, trying to maintain my composure.

"Counter offer. How about you erase the debt, and you give me a BJ instead, and I'll agree," I said, hoping to sound confident.

The man behind me put his hands on my shoulders, and I felt the pressure intensify.

"You cocky son of a bitch," Faith growled, "Okay, you are on."

Marcus hit me on the shoulder.

"What the fuck are you doing, Mike? Faith is not someone you want to fuck with."

"Don't worry, man, I got this," I said, giving him a serious look.

The dealer flipped over the next card, *Jack of diamonds*. Looking down, the cards read *Queen of Diamonds, King of*

Diamonds, Eight of Spades, Eight of Diamonds, and *Jack of Diamonds.*

Faith flips her cards one by one, first Eight of Clubs. A bead of sweat rolls down my forehead, thinking about the big, burly dude having me bent over. She flipped her other card, *Ace of Diamonds.* Dealer announced, "The lady has a flush, sir."

I knew I had won, but my heart still raced. I took a quick breath as I flipped over my cards—two Kings.

Faith's face lit up with a grin, but when I revealed the second King, her expression changed. It dropped like she'd just seen a ghost.

Marcus jumped up. "Holly shit dude!" he said, pushing the guy's hands off my shoulders.

I stared at Faith; she looked like she had seen a ghost.

"Looks like her debt is erased," I said, standing up.

"Looks that way, Mike," she replied quietly, glancing up at me.

I grabbed my chips and handed them to Marcus.

"Hey bud, can you get the money for me? Take whatever you lost from the winnings."

"Yeah, man, I got you. Appreciate it," he said, walking over to the guy who had now moved further back from the table.

"I had a great time, Faith," I said, smiling at her. But it's late… I'm gonna bounce."

As I headed for the door, Faith stepped in my path.

"Where do you think you are going?"

"I'm headed home now. If you can move, that'd be great."

"I don't think so," she said, her voice low and threatening. "I believe I have to suck your pathetic cock, as the terms of the bet."

"I was just fucking with you, don't worry about it." I tried to slide past her, but she blocked me again.

"Either you get your ass in my room yourself or I'll have one of my men drag you. I don't owe anyone, and I won't start now."

"Lead the way," I said, resigning to the inevitable, as she grabbed my hand.

CHAPTER 18

Faith led me through a maze of people, everyone dancing as though they were extras in a movie told to focus on their moves and ignore everything else around them. We reached a white bedroom door with a sign that read, Do Not Enter.

"Come on, don't be shy now, lover boy," she teased.

"I wouldn't dream of it," I replied with a smirk as we stepped inside.

The room was impeccably clean, and the LED lights on the ceiling glowed a deep red. The bed, a queen size, was centered against the back wall in front of a window. It had black silk sheets with a gray throw blanket draped across it. Three pillows rested neatly against the leather headboard.

Faith closed the door and pointed for me to sit on the bed; I did exactly that.

"Hurry and get those pants off," she demanded.

As my pants were halfway down, I heard a loud bang, and the music cut off, and people started to scream. I tried to pull my pants up, but Faith pushed me on the bed.

"Get off me, what the fuck was that Faith?" I shouted, struggling to sit up.

She ignored me and pulled a gun from the dresser near the door.

"You thought you would waltz in here, take my money, and demand that I free your friend… This isn't a movie asshole," she snapped.

I yanked my pants back up and sat against the pillows.

"It was a game, and you lost you crazy bitch," I shot back, anger boiling over.

Faith aimed and shot the pillow to my right, and I jumped in fear.

"Okay! Okay! What do you want?" I asked, my voice shaking out of fear. I grabbed a pillow as that would stop a bullet.

"I want you to learn your fucking lesson. What better way to do that than killing your friend, wouldn't you agree?"

Her words struck me like lightning.

"Marcus!" I shouted, terror gripping me.

Faith walked to my left side and put the gun to my head. Another loud bang came from the living room. The sounds of people screaming had faded, and all that was left was an uneasy silence. Faith looked toward the door as if she was expecting someone to walk in.

Seizing the moment, I shoved the pillow against the side of the gun, knocking it out of her grip and behind me. As she pulled the trigger, the bullet hit the headboard instead. Adrenaline surged through me as I shot up, grabbing Faith from behind in an attempt to wrestle her down. The struggle was chaotic, but I managed to smack the gun out of her reach. Grabbing her tightly, I lifted her off the ground and hurled her into the wooden dresser.

The mirror attached to the dresser wobbled from the impact and began to fall. I lunged forward, stopping it just before it hit her.

"I may be a lot of things, but I'm not a killer," I said with a grim smile.

Faith didn't respond at all.

"That must have knocked you out, not so tough now, are you?" I muttered, chuckling nervously before realizing I needed to get the hell out of the house.

Fortunately, there were two windows, one against the left wall that led to the side of the house and one behind the bed that led into the backyard. Jumping on the bed, I checked the backyard for people and saw three dudes talking.

"Fuck that!" I mumbled under my breath.

Opening the side window, I heard someone coming.

"Faith, that guy is dealt with. What do you want me to do now?" a voice said from behind the door.

As I climbed out of the window, I heard the door open. I bolted for my car; my heart was pounding in my chest.

I was stopped dead in my tracks as I saw through the window a dude in a black hoodie and blue jeans standing over Marcus, searching his body. My friend is on his stomach, lying in a pool of his own blood. Bastards shot him in the back like a bunch of cowards.

"Shit, shit,…" My eyes start to swell as I get a good glimpse of this asshole's face.

I squinted to get a better look at the guy standing over Marcus. He was a white dude with a bald head and a tattoo above his left eyebrow. It read *GRIM* in bold red letters.

It was fucking Kieth.

Instead of the usual rage that would've consumed me, despair and fear overtook my body. I shook uncontrollably, tears streaming down my face.

This spooked the bald bastard; he looked straight at me and dashed to the window. I ran as hard as I could to the car, fumbling with the keys as I got in and shut the door. The engine roared to life as the bald man and another from the game ran out to catch me. I put the pedal to the floor, and my tires spurned. The sound of my peel-out echoed through the neighborhood, loud enough to be heard for blocks.

In the rearview mirror, I watched them standing there, Faith shouting something inaudible at the men.

"Where do I go? What do I do? I'm so fucked. I'm so fucked," I muttered, panic and despair closing in around me.

CHAPTER 19

Swerving in and out of traffic, the tears still ran down my face like an open faucet. I flipped out my phone and started scrolling through my contacts.

"Who do I call? Who do I call? The police? Do I call Jimmy? Or Tes? Fuckkkkkkk!!" I muttered, slamming my thumb down on Jimmy's name.

"Come on, come on," (*Ring Ring Ring*) I whispered as the phone rang. "Answer the fucking phone man!"

"*Your call has been forwarded to automatic voicemail…*"

I cursed under my breath, ended the call, and immediately dialed Tes.

Two rings, and she answered. "Hey Mike, what's up?" she said casually, her tone light and unsuspecting.

"Holy shit, Tes, I just witnessed some crazy shit," I blurted, my voice trembling, my breathing erratic.

"Slow down, what's wrong? Are you okay?" Her voice comes off as slightly panicked, laced up with urgency.

"Marcus… she fucking killed Marcus," I choked out, my voice cracking as tears came down like a heavy rain.

"What!!? Marcus is dead?" she stammered, her voice breaking, disbelief and panic crashing through her words. I could hear her voice started to break up.

"That fucking dude Keith from the other night shot him… shot him in the fucking back!" I shouted, anger and guilt spilling out like venom.

The light in front of me turns red, and I blast right through it, cutting off two passing cars. Their horns honk loudly as they swerve to avoid colliding with each other.

"What was that? Are you driving? Pull the car over right now, Mike", she demanded her voice rising, firm but edged with fear.

"I can't... I can't what if they are following me!" I gasped, paranoia gripping me, my hands trembling on the wheel.

"Mike, relax and look in your mirror. Do you see anyone following you?" she asked, her tone softening but still steady, trying to keep me grounded.

I took a look, and there was nothing beyond me but empty streets and half-lit street lamps.

Taking a breath and slowing down. The tears dry up and my heart slows. Nothing made sense. How could this have happened? I realized I was still on the phone when I heard Tes's voice again, sharper this time.

"Tell me where you are, and I'll meet you there," she said firmly, her determination slicing through the haze in my head.

"No... it's not safe. I don't know what to do," I admitted, my voice small, weighed down by fear and guilt.

Her words brought me comfort like everything will be alright. I pulled the car into an alleyway next to a popular fast-food restaurant; I used to go there all the time with my mom when I was a kid.

"Mike," she said, her voice soothing now, like a balm over a fresh wound, "If you don't tell me where you are, I'll walk around until I find you."

She sounded serious; I knew she really would. Reluctantly, I gave in. I hit the steering wheel and sighed loudly.

"I'm right next to *Big Cheese,* the one by Wat's drug store; I'm in the joining ally," I muttered, defeated.

"I'll be there in like five minutes. Have a smoke, and just calm down. We'll figure this out," she said, her words steady and reassuring like she really believed we could fix it.

CLICK

The phone call ended, and I threw my phone into the glove compartment in frustration. It bounced off and landed in the foot well. My friend was just murdered because I was high and playing around with a fucking monster like I was someone strong and capable of handling any adult situation. Frustration boiled inside me. The guilt hit me like a tidal wave. How could I ever face his family and admit this was my fault? Marcus was such a good dude, and he's dead because of my actions. What do I do? How do I tell his family it was my fault? The tears started again while I fumbled with the pack of cigarettes I had in my cupholder.

The cigarette I put in my mouth, now wet from tears, struggles to light under the flame of my lighter. But it gave way, and I took a large puff and finally released it.

Shocker! It didn't make me feel any better. I took another puff before chucking it out the window. I needed something harder; I needed something to take away this guilt and suffering. I rummaged through my center console and the glove box but found nothing.

Until I remembered I had a stash hidden underneath the spare tire in the trunk for rare moments of desperation. Taking the keys out of the engine and stepping out into the dark alley, I rushed toward the truck.

In the middle of such a horrible situation, I dropped the keys as I tried to unlock the trunk. As I bid to pick them up, I banged my head, trying to stand.

"Why? Why is this happening?" I muttered, tears blurring my vision again.

Finally, I unlocked the drunk and grabbed the red leather-skinned stash kit; I opened it up and sat on the ground. I dumped it all out on the pavement; I had a bag of perks, weed, and coke. I didn't want to feel this pain anymore; I just wanted to be numb.

My hands hovered over the stash, but all I could see was Marcus—his face laughing and then his body, lifeless and bloodied, still warm. I loosed it, crushed the pills, and dumped the powder on the ground. I do the same for the others as well. If I wasn't that high and fucking arrogant, he would still be here.

I slumped to the ground, knees pulled tight to my chest, feeling like the child I knew I was deep down. I sat there, broken, waiting for someone—anyone—to save me from the mess I'd made.

CHAPTER 20

"Michael... Michael."

I woke up with a deep breath. It felt colder than it did before I cried myself to sleep sitting on the pavement moments ago. My vision was blurred, and my head was heavy, but her voice brought some clarity. I could also hear someone else in the distance, speaking from a car parked at the mouth of the alley.

"Tes, is Micheal okay? What's going on? You want me to come over there and help?" The voice sounded so familiar, but my mind was still foggy.

"I'm good; I just gotta stand up," I mumbled, using the car as leverage to haul myself upright. My limbs felt like lead, but I managed to steady myself.

I hugged Tes tight; the smell of her leave-in conditioner weirdly calmed me. Lavender. Her body felt warm, and the killer hoodie she was wearing felt super soft. Looking over her shoulder, all I saw was headlights and a silhouette.

I let Tes go and shout over in a not-so-loud, loud voice. "Jimmy? Is that you?"

"Yeah, brother, it's me," Jimmy replied, his tone calm but cautious. "Tes told me to hang back by the car until she made sure you were okay."

"I called… Never mind," I muttered, my words trailing off. *Was he with Tes, and that's why he didn't answer? What were they doing?* My mind raced with questions I didn't have the energy to process.

I stopped my thought process and looked into Tes's amazing brown eyes.

“This all my fault. I got high and thought I was untouchable, and they killed Marcus. They fucking shot him, Tes,”

Tes hugged me again, leaned her mouth near my ear and whispered, “I’m not gonna lie to you; you do play a role in his death, but Faith and Keith are bad people. Don’t put the blame entirely on yourself.” Her words cut me straight through to the bone. For some reason, I thought she’d say it wasn’t my fault, that it was just all Faith, and that I shouldn’t feel guilty for Marcus’s death.

Jimmy approached, resting a hand on my shoulder. “Dude, I loved Marcus too, but he was an adult. He knew who Faith was,” he said gently.

Moving back from Tes, I slapped Jimmy’s hand off of me, “What the hell are you talking about? He was our friend, and my stupid, ignorant ass got him killed.”

Jimmy squared up, his fists clenched like he was ready to throw a punch. I charged toward him, but Tes quickly stepped between us, her eyes filled with disappointment. The look hit harder than a fist ever could.

“By the way, Jimmy,” I spat, my voice dripping with venom, “Friend, I fucking called you, and you sent me to voicemail, and then you showed up with Tes? Care to explain this?”

Tes looked genuinely taken off guard and the look in her eyes was like she just saw a ghost. Jimmy, however, still looked like he wanted to rip my head off.

“I know you are feeling guilty,” Tes said, her voice trembling slightly. “But that’s no reason to go and try fighting a friend that showed up for you.”

"Mike, you must be high as hell," Jimmy sneered, his smirk infuriating. He motioned toward the mess of powder and crushed pills on the ground. "I see all the shit you spilled. Must have had a lot of shit to make a mess that big."

"No.., No, I didn't take anything," I insisted, shaking my head, "I poured it all out."

Tes and Jimmy both had a facial expression that clearly looked like they didn't believe me. Why would they? I'm just a drug-taken party, hard, good time, dude.

"It's okay, Mike," Tes said, patting my shoulder. Her voice was kind but laced with pity. "Even if you did, Mike, you just went through some heavy shit."

"I'm fucking telling you the truth," I said, my voice rising in frustration. "How did he get to you so fast, Tes? He lives 20 minutes from you, and it took you 15 mins to get here."

Jimmy stepped back, his face shifting as he tried to explain. "Truth is, man, I work with Tes. She can tell you the rest, but can we get out of this disgusting alley? The smell of this fast food is making me sick." He spat on the ground, his expression sour.

"Damn it, Jimmy," Tes snapped, flicking her wrist in frustration, her bracelets jangling noisily. "What's wrong with you, man? We are dealing with an actual shit, and you have to feed into this bullshit; just take off, man."

Jimmy hesitated, then threw up his hands. "Call me later, man; if you need something, I got you," he said, waving before climbing into his car. He drove off, leaving Tes and me alone as the sun began to rise, its light slowly peeling back the darkness of the alley.

Tes and I were face to face. The sun was starting to rise now, and the dark alley doesn't look so dark anymore.

I turned to Tes, my shoulders sagging with exhaustion. "Tes, I really want to know what he's talking about, but I don't think I can handle that right now. Can we just find a place to sleep?"

"Of course, babe," she said, giving me a sad smile. It was full of pity and sadness, but somehow still the most beautiful smile I'd ever seen.

The wind started to howl as I opened the car door for her and shut it once she was completely in the car. I gave her a weak smile, a silent reassurance that I was okay, or at least trying to be.

"Where do we go? I can't go to the police. She'll kill everyone I love, and I don't want to go home." I said my voice barely above a whisper.

Tes reached over and grabbed my hand, leaned her head on my shoulder, and looked up, "I know a place, it's safe and I actually think it'll help explain the Jimmy situation. It's right off of Strawberry Street. Nice to the abandoned gas station."

"I know the place," I murmured, starting the engine.

Tes grabbed her phone and started to text someone as I pulled off. Her face was illuminated by the soft glow of her phone screen.

I glanced at her, my heart heavy but grateful. *I'm so lucky to have this girl in my life right now.*

CHAPTER 21

"Home" by Good Neighbors played on the radio, the wind coming through the open windows, the sun rising, and last but not least, Tes's hand in mine. At that moment, it was like the previous night had never happened.

It has only been a short period of time since I've met Tes but it felt like nothing I've ever felt. The feeling of being wanted and the feeling that she felt the same way was enough to move the world. I tightened my grip on her hand gently and locked eyes with her, and she smiled.

As we pulled onto *Strawberry St.*, I reached to turn the music down. But Tes stopped me. As we turned onto Strawberry Street, I reached for the volume knob to lower the music, but Tes stopped me, placing her hand over mine. "Just let the song finish, okay?" she said, her expression wistful as if she were trying to hold onto this fragile moment for just a little longer.

I leaned back and just let the scene play out some romantic type. How did I get here? My dad had completely set me up: money, house, and car, and all I had to do was grow the hell up, and I would have had an amazing life. Instead, I disrespected my mother and stepdad, did drugs whenever I had the chance, and fucked off. At the end of the day, I was the man who never grew up and blamed everyone else for my problems.

"Hey," I said, breaking the silence. "After this, I need to go to my mom's; I just… I just need to tell her what happened; I feel like you and her are the only people I can trust."

The song faded as Tes opened the door and stepped out of the car. I followed, the cool morning air hitting my face like a wake-up call.

"I understand," she said softly, motioning for me to follow her.

Tes grabbed her phone, and again, she was texting someone. She led me to a trashy shit-hole house that looked like it had been abandoned for more than twenty years. The stench of urine and decay hung heavy in the air, making my stomach churn.

"Tes, what the hell are we doing here?" I stopped walking in the middle of the one-way street, tugging on her hand to halt her, too.

"This where I made a massive mistake Micheal," she said, her voice shaky. She hesitated, then continued, "You see, I'm an artist, right? Well… it's more of a graffiti… You have seen my room." She paused, looking like she was on the verge of tears.

"Yeah," I said gently, brushing a strand of hair from her face and cupping the back of her head. "You are amazing. But how does that equate to you making a massive mistake?"

Her eyes filled with shame as she looked away. "Well, one night, I was tagging, and I came across a haul truck. The back was open so I decided to tag the side of it. Not five minutes later, two police officers caught me."

She knelt down and took a seat on the curb. I quickly took a seat next to her and put my hand around her.

"Okay… So what happened after that," I asked, keeping my voice steady.

"Well, the cops let me go with a warning," she said, her voice trembling. "But when the other cop was checking out the rest of the truck, he found a bunch of coke in the back."

I frowned, trying to piece it together. "And how does that tie you in with Jimmy? I don't understand, Tes."

Tes took my arm off of her, stood up, and started to pace in front of me. She visibly looked nervous.

"Mike," she said, her voice cracking, "The truck belonged to Faith. She found out that they impounded the truck, and it was my fault," She rubbed the back of her head anxiously.

"Okay, so she found out how?" I asked, rising to my feet.

"Well… I guess the cops had released a report about it because it was a big find and they said that it was me in the paper. They called me a 'Good Samaritan'. They made up a story about how I called them, which is bullshit, then Faith tracked me down,"

She stopped pacing and knelt down in front of me, taking my hand in hers. "Faith gave me three options: pay her back the money she lost, work for her, or…" Her voice faltered. "Or get gang-raped and then cut into pieces. I chose to work for her."

The shock overtook my face, and panic set in. My heart started to beat faster than it ever had.

"Oh fuck, Tes!" I whispered, panic thick in my voice, "How does Jimmy play into this shit?"

Tes stood up, holding my hand, prompting me to stand up. She looked deep into my eyes and was quiet for about a minute.

"I don't know Jimmy's situation," she admitted finally. "But he and I run drugs for Faith. There is no end in sight for me. I'm sorry for being super secretive about me and Jimmy. But I swear, there's nothing between us. Nothing sexual, at least."

I started walking back to the car and looked over my shoulder, "I want to go home… Do you wanna come with me?"

Tes grabbed my hand, and we headed to the car; the sun was high in the sky, the smell of the dirty streets, and the overwhelming feeling like my life was fucked enough to call it quits.

We jumped in the car started it up, and looked at her, "Anything else you wanna tell me? Last chance, to be honest," I winked, trying to lighten the mood just a little.

She smiled faintly, her eyes tired. "Well… you know that graffiti artist Zero-G? The G stands for grief."

I chuckled despite myself. "I did think your work on your walls looked familiar," I smiled.

She looked out the window, her voice soft but determined. "Once this thing with Faith is over, I'm gonna get out of here; there's this art program in NY. That's where I'm going."

"I'll do whatever I can to help you, Tes," I promised, my voice firm.

"I know," she whispered.

We drove off toward my house, the wind rushing through the windows, the music blasting, and the weight of everything unspoken pressing down on us. A storm was coming, and we both knew it.

CHAPTER 22

Lying in bed with Tes passed out next to me used to bring me comfort but now all I could do was to think about how screwed we both were.

My ceiling started to look stranger with every passing moment; the more I stared at it, the stranger it got. My restless mind warped it into twisted daydreams of Marcus's murder and Tes's tangled mess. The fact that Tes was my favorite street artist should have excited me, but all I could focus on was how she and Jimmy had kept me in the dark about their dangerous lives. I wanted to help her, but I had to help myself first.

I got up slowly, not to wake Tes, and threw on my blue jeans and my black noir hoodie. No shirt underneath. I put on ankle socks and my vans and headed out of the door.

I flipped my phone open and realized I had three missed calls from my mom and two from my stepdad. But I decided not to call the back and to just head over to their house, figure I could smooth things out with them, and then go talk to Jimmy about that Tes shit.

My car rumbled softly to life as I pulled away, careful not to disturb the neighbors. The streets were quiet, almost unnervingly so, as I made my way to my mother's house. I got to my mother's in a short time and pulled into the driveway behind Old Reliable. My mother lived in a double-wide trailer on a small piece of land my grandfather had left when he passed. It was a decent trailer with its yellow siding, black roof, and black shutters.

My mother always prided herself on her garden. It was actually pretty nice. She had tulips and large sunflowers guarded by yard gnomes. Vibrant tulips and towering sunflowers swayed in the breeze, guarded by an odd collection of gnomes: a fisherman, a biker, a hippie, and even a Mr. Bean lookalike. I smiled faintly, remembering the time I broke her Marilyn Monroe gnome—the one in the iconic white dress. She had been furious.

When I got to the front door, I hesitated. I always got nervous about bringing bad things to my mom, but who else could I go to? I knocked on the door lightly, praying for some reason that they didn't hear it, and it gave me an excuse to leave.

At the end of the knock, the door swung open, and my stepdad Harvey stood in the middle of the doorway. Harvey was a big guy, 6'2, always dressed like the main character from Home Improvement. He had got on a lumberjack button down and blue jeans and white socks, and his hair was neatly combed; bread was wild, though.

"Well, if it isn't the prodigal son," he said with a smirk, crossing his arms. "Finally decided to visit. Must mean something's wrong."

I scuffed and put my hand out.

"Good to see you, Harv. Mom inside?"

He grabbed my hand firmly and shook it. The look in his eyes was different than normal.

"Yeah, she's in the living room. She'll be happy you stopped by, come on in,"

He stepped back from the main door and waited for me to pass so that he could shut the door behind me.

Stepping inside, the familiar scent of apples and vanilla wrapped around me like a warm hug. The walls were lined with trinkets and photos from their vacations—miniature lighthouses, seashell frames, and even a cuckoo clock I'd always found oddly comforting. As I walked through the living room, my gaze lingered on the red stain on the white carpet—a permanent reminder of the Kool-Aid disaster from my childhood.

Looking forward, Mom was sitting on a white, worn leather couch covered in a white fuzzy blanket with a bunch of pictures of all three of us on it.

"Hey mom, how are you?" I said, scratching the back of my head in a bit of nervousness.

She jumped up and hugged me.

"Michael!" she exclaimed, jumping to her feet and wrapping me in a tight hug. "It's so good to see you. I wasn't expecting you today!" she let go and patted the seat right next to her. I took a seat and started looking at the TV in front of me. They were watching the show where they buy storage lockers and try to resale the items. I never really minded the show.

"Well, you called a few times, so I figured I'd stop by." I smiled

"Oh yeah, I was just calling to see if you'd work on the car for me," she said, brushing her hand over mine. "It's been acting funny."

"I can't today, but I will take a look soon, just have a lot going on."

Harvey chuckled as he settled into his recliner.

"You? A lot going on? Like what?" His smirk was infuriating.

"Harvey, stop it! He's allowed to have stuff going on." she laughed

Harvey leaned forward, his expression softening. "What's really going on, kid? You don't look like yourself."

I stared at the floor, the weight of everything crashing down on me. Suddenly, the tears came, heavy and unrelenting. My shoulders shook as I buried my face in my hands, the sobs echoing in the room.

"So much has happened," I choked out. "I'm sorry, you guys. I realize how wrong I've been and how irresponsible I've acted."

Both of them, shocked, started to speak at the same time, but Harvey let Mom go first. Mom's hand flew to her mouth, her eyes wide with concern. Harvey leaned closer, his large hand gripping my shoulder.

"Honey, you've been acting wild for a little while, but it's nothing that you can't fix."

Harvey sat next to me.

"Listen, whatever it is, we'll help. Is it money? Did you get someone pregnant?" Harvey asked with a concerning tone.

I threw out a little sop laughter for the ridiculous pregnant comment but realized this was not a great time to laugh.

"I've been acting untouchable—like nothing could happen to me. I've done drugs, drank too much, fought for no reason... I treated people like crap that I can't see, and now I'm heading down a bad path."

Both were completely silent as I sobbed and went on.

"I thought I could help a friend, not because they needed me to help but because I thought nothing bad could happen to me, and I got a close friend killed."

Their stunned silence hung heavy in the air. Mom's hand trembled as she placed it on my knee.

"What, who died? Tell me right now, Michael!!" My mother asked sternly; in my mind, I knew this tone; that was her angry tone.

"Tell us, Michael," Harvey urged, his voice firm but calm.

Through sobs, I told them everything—the drugs, the fights, Marcus's murder, Tes's mess. By the time I finished, Mom and Harvey were both on their feet, pacing with expressions of disbelief and heartbreak.

Mom's voice was low, almost a whisper. "Michael, I... I don't even know what to say. I'm so sorry about your friend. But you can't go to the police. That woman—Faith— she'll find us. She'll come here."

Harvey walked out of the room, heading to their bedroom.

"What were you thinking?" Mom asked, tears streaming down her face. "Why would you put yourself in that position?"

"I don't know mom, I just wanted to help a friend, I thought, but I'm thinking now it was all pride and not as selfless as I thought,"

Harvey returned and grabbed me by the arm; I didn't fight back. He pulled me to the door and opened it.

"Harvey, wait," Mom pleaded, following us.

At the door, Harvey handed me the bag. His voice softened as he looked me in the eye.

"Take this and be careful; I am proud of you for finally realizing your actions have consequences. Be safe and contact us often. We love you. I love you."

Mom started crying and told me that she loved me.

"I love you guys too; sorry if my way of living has disappointed you. It was never my intention."

They stood in the doorway as I climbed into my car. As I drove away, I glanced back to see Mom holding onto Harvey, their silhouettes framed by the soft glow of the porch light.

CHAPTER 23

My eyes started to well up again as I reached the stop sign up the road from my mothers. What do I do? Damn, I need to go see Jimmy.

I glanced over at the bag Harvey had handed me, the curiosity finally too much to ignore. Tugging at the drawstrings, I opened it to find a box of ammo and a black Glock 22 nestled inside. I had to give it to Harvey. At least he was trying to protect me. I dropped the magazine and did a round check. Mags full but no round in the chamber. I loaded the 22 and set it in my seat.

With a deep breath, I hit the gas and headed toward Jimmy's place. It wasn't far—just a quick five-minute drive—but my thoughts made the journey feel longer.

When I pulled up, Jimmy's navy blue Chevy Nova was parked haphazardly in the yard instead of the driveway. Classic Jimmy. I parked at the curb, grabbed the gun, and tucked it into the small of my back. With a deep breath, I stepped out and approached the door.

KNOCK KNOCK KNOCK

I could hear Jimmy stumbling toward the door

KNOCK KNOCK KNOCK

"Fuck I'm coming… I'm coming. Hold on!"

I heard the sounds of locks and bolts unlocking.

The door swung open, and Jimmy was standing there, not wearing any pants. He has a white hoodie and a black beanie but no pants.

"Yo, what the actual hell, man?" I groaned, shielding my eyes.

"What's up, Mike? You wanna come in or what?" he asked casually, turning and walking back into the house like it was just another Tuesday.

"Yeah, I guess. But, for God's sake, put on some damn pants," I muttered, stepping inside.

Jimmy sat down on the sofa and started to roll a joint

"Mike, you know I'm always glad to hang out, but why are you here?"

"I need to know more about you and Tes," I said, crossing my arms. "Why the hell didn't you tell me what kind of mess you two were mixed up in?"

Jimmy shrugged, not even looking up from his task. "I didn't think it was important, man, like we run drugs for faith, no big deal, so does half of this fucking town."

I sighed and took a seat. "How long have you actually known Tes?"

He paused, thinking. "I dunno… a couple months longer than you, maybe." He licked the paper and sealed the joint. "We just figured you'd overreact. You have a tendency to do that," he added with a laugh.

"Dude, I'm screwed… What the hell am I going to do?" I nervously shook my leg.

Jimmy lit the joint, took a slow drag, and coughed out a cloud of smoke. "I don't know, man, how about sit there, smoke up with me, and try to relax," He extended the joint toward me, but I waved it off.

"Nah! I'm good, man. I've got to stay clear-headed, gotta find a way out of this."

Jimmy leaned back, exhaling another plume of smoke. "There's only two ways out of this, brother. You either kill her… or you run. Cops ain't an option. If you go to them, Faith will find your family and make you regret it."

"Yeah, your right!" I leaned back and looked at the ceiling.

Not too long ago, I had what I thought of as a perfect life; I guess it wasn't so perfect.

"Listen, Jim," I began, "this life… it isn't what I thought it was. The drugs, the partying—it doesn't hit the same anymore. We're not kids. This shit's getting old."

Jimmy snorted, "Maybe for you, man; I never really understood why you acted the way you did. I mean you've got money and a house and options. I live like this because I have to."

"You could do something else, though, man!" I countered, meeting his eyes.

"No, man, I'm a high school dropout who's High 100% of the time; moving drugs is the only way I'm gonna make enough money, and I've made my peace with that."

I sighed and pulled the Glock from my waistband, staring at it in my hands.

"Damn! So you are gonna kill her, Mike, not really like you!"

"Harvey gave it to me," I said quickly. "It's just for protection. I'm not gonna kill her."

As if on cue, my phone buzzed in my hoodie pocket. I pulled it out and checked the screen. Tes. Shit.

"You hold on; I have to take this," I got up and walked back to the front door.

I hit the green answer button and put it to my ear.

"Hey babe, what's up?" I try not to sound rattled.

"Hey," Tes said, her voice tinged with worry. "I woke up, and you were gone. Are you alright? Where did you go?"

"I'm good," I lied. "Stopped by my mom's, and now I'm at Jimmy's. Just needed to talk some things out, figure out my next move."

"What did Jimmy say?" Her voice worried

"He said to kill her or run. I don't think I can kill her, Tes. I just don't think I have it in me." I admitted.

"Then let's run," she said firmly. "You and me. We can go to New York and start over. Leave all this behind."

I hesitated, her words stirring a strange mix of hope and doubt. "Yeah! And I can have my mom sell my house, and she can send me the money. We can take the car and the cash I have on hand and go."

"Mike, we're both in bad situations, but we can have a happy life together," her voice sounds sturdy.

"Okay, babe, when I get back, we'll leave first thing. Can you start backing my things?"

"Of course. Can you stop by my place and grab my stuff? It's all in a red and purple go bag in my closet. It has all my important things."

"Uhm, Yeah, I can definitely stop and grab it; got to go, babe."

"Be safe. I'll see you soon; I love you."

"I... I love you too..."

Sliding the phone back into my pocket, I returned to the living room. Jimmy had finally put on pants, thank God. He walked over and pulled me into a tight hug.

"I'm sorry, but I overheard; I'm going to miss you, bother," he said, his voice cracking.

I hugged him back and took a step away from him.

"I'm gonna miss you too, man; sorry for hassling you about the Tes stuff."

"No swear, brother, be careful. I hope to see you again!"

He let me go and walked me to the door, the joint still smoldering between his fingers.

As I stepped outside, he leaned against the doorframe and called out, "I'll see you around, bud."

I nodded, climbing into my car. "Yeah, I'll see you."

CHAPTER 24

I kept the radio off while I took the drive to Tes's house. Were we really going to do this, leave everything behind? I feel like we'd be happy together, but we just met not too long ago. Could we really do this? What if we moved out there and things don't work out? Then I'm stuck in New York all alone. I guess it beats being dead, though, so that's a plus.

The streets were nearly empty, and the sun hung high in the sky, casting its harsh light on everything. The glare from the storefront windows danced in streaks along my car, putting on a kaleidoscopic little show as I passed. It didn't bother me, though. Strangely, it felt almost comforting. I used to think I ruled this town, but now? Now, I felt like I'd been the jester all along, and the joke had always been on me.

The street covered in artwork from Zero-G made me smile as I pulled up to Tes's apartment. Before hopping out, I took my phone out and messaged Tes.

Hey, just got to your apartment. Be about another hour. See you soon.

I hopped out and saw the same cat from before. He curled around my leg and purred as I knelt down to pet him.

"Hey there, little buddy. How've you been, huh?" I murmured, smiling as it stretched lazily in front of me before scampering off.

I rang the doorbell and glanced up at the window, waiting. Nothing. After about two minutes, I rang again, knocking this time for good measure. Still no answer. Testing the door handle, I realized it was unlocked. Slowly, I pushed the door open.

"Yo, anyone home!! It's like I just have to grab something for Tes real quick!"

The place was quiet—eerily so. I moved toward the stairs, taking each creaky step with caution. The air upstairs was thick with the stale smell of weed and old alcohol, though the place itself looked cleaner than I remembered. Way cleaner, actually. It almost looked like they were prepping for an inspection or something. I felt a twinge of guilt for keeping my shoes on as I moved toward the living room.

Walking further into the living room and looking around, I noticed a piece of printer paper on the glass coffee table.

Hey Tes, we've all decided to go on a trip to Vegas at the last minute. Tiger's idea. Think we'll be back in about a week, but who knows? Call us if you need anything—you know we got you, girl.

Love, the gang.

Damn, that sounds like a good time; I wish I were with them. I put the note in my pocket and headed to her room. As I opened the door, I immediately noticed her room was spotless. Seeing her bed, I needed to sit down; everything was moving way too fast. I took a seat on the bed and laid back; the warm, familiar comforters reminded me of the first day I woke in Tes's room. The smell and the blinding headache are not there this time; I'm not so sure that's a good thing. Looking around, I noticed the graffiti on the walls was covered with a fresh coat of black paint. And the carpets looked recently cleaned.

"Why would she paint over her art like that?" I muttered, frowning. It had been so good. I couldn't understand it.

As I sat on the bed, I started to recount all the moments I'd had in this town. There were some bad, but damn, those were their good times. The feeling of reckless abandonment as I tore my way through life and the friends I made along the way were top-notch.

Shaking it off, I stood up and walked to the closet. Opening the door, I saw the bag hanging off a hook, just where Tes said it would be. It was a large purple and red backpack, and when I lifted it, its weight caught me off guard.

"Jeez, Tes, what do you have in here?" I mumbled to myself, slinging it over my shoulder.

I threw it on my back and stepped out the door, closing it behind me. The thought of spending the rest of my life with Tes completely engulfed my mind as I went out to the car. Sitting in the driver seat, I tossed the bag in the back, and once again, the engine roared to life. Free Bird by Lynyrd Skynyrd came on the radio. I turned up the volume, letting the song fill the car as I drove, the 13-minute ride feeling like both an eternity and the blink of an eye.

CHAPTER 25

Pulling slowly into the driveway, I realized how crazy that was. I was running from a group of thugs, my friend was dead, my step-father gave me a gun, and Tes was starting a new life with me in NYC.

Shutting off the car, I stayed there, staring at the house. Part of me hoped I'd wake up any second, realizing this was just some messed-up dream or a bad trip.

The top-floor window curtain moved, and my eyes darted up. Tes was looking at me through the glass, and her expression was not an excited one, which threw me off.

The gun is cool to the touch as I grab it. The weight of the gun swung as I headed to the front door back and forth like a pendulum. Tes opened the door for me as I reached it. She looked now happier to see me until she noticed the gun in my hand.

"Mike, where did you get that gun?" she asked, her voice sharp and filled with alarm.

She reached for it, but I instinctively pulled my arm back, holding it out of her reach.

"My stepdad gave it to me," I said firmly. "For protection."

I stepped past her and headed straight for the bedroom to pack my things. Her footsteps followed close behind, but something about her energy felt off—nervous, almost jumpy. My eyes darted to the bags by the door of her room, already packed, and a strange knot formed in my stomach.

"Tes, why were your bags already packed, and why was your room painted and cleaned."

She stopped and grabbed my hand, and I turned and faced her right outside the bedroom.

"Mike, I was planning on leaving already; there's an art program in NY that I was accepted into. I'm not happy you are in this situation, but I'm happy you're coming with me."

I sighed, letting her words sink in. My arms wrapped around her as I pulled her into a hug.

"I understand; this gonna be a fresh start for both of us; I know we can make it."

I broke the hug, leaning in to kiss her deeply. Her hands slid down my arms as we kissed, her touch soft and hesitant. Then, slowly, her fingers wrapped around the gun, and I let it go, releasing it into her grasp.

"It's you and me against the world babe!" I said with a faint smile

I turned and headed into the room, I reached my hand for the door and opened it.

Sitting on the bed in front of me was Faith, dressed in an all-black outfit, her legs crossed elegantly. Beside her stood Keith, his towering frame stiff in a blue button-down shirt and black jeans. The sight of them hit me like a gut punch, sending a spike of panic up my spine.

"Oh, shit," I breathed. "Faith? Tes, shoot that bitch!"

I spun around, but my heart sank as I saw Tes aiming the gun—straight at me. Her hands trembled, and her face was a mask of panic and despair. The look of sheer panic and desperation was on her face as she walked further into the room at gunpoint.

Faith tapped her leg with a cigarette lighter.

"What did you think you could run and hide from me, sweet Micheal?" she purred, her voice dripping with mockery.

From a black leather case, she pulled out two cigarettes, tossing one onto the ground in front of me.

"While you pick that up, you can get down on your knees in front of me," she laughed.

Her laugh echoed through the room, cold and cruel.

Jaw clenched, I sank to my knees, picking up the cigarette. Tes pressed the barrel of the gun to the back of my head, the metal icy against my skin. My chest tightened as the reality of her betrayal sank in.

"Tes," I said, my voice cracking. "What the fuck? It was supposed to be you and me."

Behind me, I heard her start to sob. Her words came out in broken gasps.

"I… I'm so sorry, Mike. It was either get chased my whole life or give you up!" She choked out.

I raised my hand toward Faith, gesturing for the lighter. She lit her own cigarette with a flick of her wrist, then tossed the lighter to me. I caught it, sparking the flame as I lit the cigarette clenched between my teeth. I glanced over at Keith, who stood there silently, like some hulking bodyguard.

"What's up, big guy?" I muttered, exhaling a puff of smoke.

He grunted as I tossed the lighter back to Faith.

"You really gonna let Tes go if she kills me? It doesn't seem like you," I smiled as I blew a cloud of smoke out.

"I am a *Businesswoman, Micheal; she does this. She's free to go,* of course!" she said smoothly.

I moved my head back against the gun and looked over my shoulder at Tes.

"Tes," I said softly, "I really do understand, and I hope you have the best career."

"Shut up, Mike!" she screamed, her voice breaking as sobs racked her body. "Just shut up and face forward!"

I took another long drag, letting the smoke fill my lungs before blowing it out in a slow, deliberate stream.

"Well," I said with a faint, bitter smile, "I guess you win this one, Faith!"

As I blew the smoke out for the last time.

"What a fucking ride!"

The last thing I heard was the metallic click of the gun.

www.ingramcontent.com/pod-product-compliance
Lightning Source LLC
Chambersburg PA
CBHW040835010826
48978CB00012BB/763